PLAYING
WITH FIRE

BY: SHERRY D. FICKLIN

Sidge 2.0
00101101001101
But when you read it backwards...

Playing With Fire
Copyright ©2015 Sherry D. Ficklin
All rights reserved.

ISBN: 978-1-63422-119-1
Cover Design by: Marya Heiman
Typography by: Courtney Nuckels
Editing by: Cynthia Shepp

For more information about our content disclosure, please utilize the QR code above with your smart phone or visit us at

www.CleanTeenPublishing.com.

ONE

IN MY DREAM, I'M DROWNING. IT'S NOT THE FIRST time. Hell, it's not the one-hundredth time. Even as I blink away the last dying fragments of the nightmare, I can still feel the cold water clinging to my skin. I look down to see my arms shining with sweat.

Around me, the car hums, the gentle vibration of tires on asphalt trying to lull me back to sleep. Travel far enough for long enough, and you develop the uncanny ability to sleep anywhere. Like in a crowded plane, on a noisy bus, even in a two-door rental sedan while your father drives down Highway 70 like he's being chased by armed assassins.

I force myself awake, stretching as much as I'm able to in the cramped car. Reaching for the cooler behind my seat, I pull out a Red Bull and crack it open. Dad doesn't say anything, even though I know he hates me drinking them. I can't tell if he's just distracted by the road or if he's finally given up the fight against my caffeine addiction.

When I've gulped down half the can, he points out my window to a small, wooden sign that reads, *Welcome to Havelock. Pardon our noise. It's the sound of freedom.*

"We're almost there," he says, as if I should be excited.

Truth is, I kind of am. Sure, I'll miss the blistering hot summers and barren deserts of Arizona... oh wait, no. No, I won't. Not even a little. I won't miss the heat—and whoever coined the term dry heat should be shot in the head—I won't miss the crappy little town, and I sure as hell won't miss my friends. Or the people I used to call friends, I should say.

This move might as well be a prison break, as far as I'm concerned. There were worse places we could have ended up besides the small, coastal North Carolina town. There were better places too, but hey, beggars can't be choosers.

When we pull up to the gate to the base, I notice a Harrier on display to my right. It's angled so it looks like it is just about to land. Or crash. I can't decide which. The guard, looking perfectly disguised in his dark green camouflage uniform, takes one look at the ID badge Dad flashes out the window, salutes, and raises the gate, letting us pass through.

We drive in what feels like circles until finally pulling into a skinny driveway.

"You have got to be joking," I whine. Marine Corps Air Station Cherry Point boasts stunning, seaside officer housing. I know—I'd looked it up online. Tall, spacious homes overlooking the ocean with big windows and hardwood floors, all generously loaned to the officers stationed there, free of charge. What I'm looking at now is *so* not on the brochure.

Being a military kid, I've lived in a lot of places, seen a lot of things. I've seen impoverished towns in Okinawa and Nigeria. I've seen entire communities made of straw shacks with one communal outhouse. None of that has prepared me for what I'm seeing now—the lowest form of civilization.

Enlisted housing, aka puke-brown duplex houses with metal windows and cheap, brown doors left over from the 1950s. There's a patch of what at first glance looks like grass but upon further inspection turns out to be shredded newspaper painted green.

I swing a glare at Dad as if lasers might shoot out of my eyes and vaporize him on the spot.

He just shrugs. "Sorry, Farris, I know it doesn't look like much, but officer housing is full because of the renovations. They have some new places coming open that we should be able to get into in about three months."

I snort. "Three months? What, did they bring in the Army Corps of Engineers?"

"Worse. Civilian contractors."

I make a horrified face, and he grins.

My father walks around the car, popping open

the trunk and tossing my worn green duffel bag into my arms. "But we can make do. I mean, we've been through worse, right kid?"

I'm not sure if he's talking about the summer we spent in a tent in San Paolo or the two weeks I just spent at my Great-Aunt Penelope's place in Kansas, which I'm actually pretty sure is some kind of portal to hell. She has a tiny condo in an "active seniors" community. Aunt P is sweet and all, but there's only so much knitting and bridge club a girl can take before she tries to drown herself in the walk-in bathtub.

I shake it all off, pushing everything down inside myself. *It's a clean slate*, I remind myself. *A chance to start over. Maybe do things right this time.* "Sure, Dad."

Dad came ahead to North Carolina to get the house set up and get things situated before rescuing me from Aunt P's place. At almost seventeen, I'm old enough to stay on my own for a few weeks if I need to, and I'd lobbied hard to do just that. But Dad isn't big on trust these days. I suppose I deserve that, really.

From the looks of things, he hasn't gotten far with the set up. When he opens the front door, I see that the house is still stuffed with boxes, piles of brown packing paper, and empty takeout containers. I kick one aside as I enter.

"Your room is over there," he says, pointing down

the hall.

I pull my shoulders back, resigned to sleeping on the floor for a few nights, but when I push the door open, I see my room is mostly set up. My bed, desk, and dresser, at least. Of course, it has the same bubblegum-pink bedspread and curtains I've had since I was nine, but still, it feels a little like home. I toss my duffel bag on the bed and am rewarded with a familiar creak.

"Thanks, Dad."

He brushes past me, bringing in my oversized suitcase and depositing it beside the empty closet. "I'm sorry I didn't get more done. Things are already piling up at work."

I can't say I'm surprised. One of the biggest reasons we landed here was Dad's ability to fix any mess—well, any mess but me—and from what he's told me, this squadron is in one helluva mess. "Is there anything I can help with?" I ask, looking around.

"It's late, kid, and you have school tomorrow."

I groan. "I slept in the car. Besides, I've got too much nervous energy to sleep. Tonight, I work," I say in my best soldier voice. "For tomorrow, I die."

Dad frowns. "Yes, high school. A fate worse than death." With a derisive snort, he turns and marches down the hall and out of sight.

"Do you even remember high school? It isn't all egg creams and sock hops anymore," I call after him.

"Now it's more metal detectors and drug dogs."

I turn away, unzipping my sack and digging around inside until my hand finds the cool metal edges of a picture frame. Pulling it out, I carefully set it up on the edge of my dresser. My mom grins out at me from the old photo. It's of us at my first middle school dance—which she'd chaperoned, of course. My dress is violet and black and flounces around my knees. She'd spent weeks sewing it for me. I touch her picture gently, trying to hold the sound of her voice in my head, just a moment longer. But it's gone as quickly as it comes, leaving me with watery eyes and a knot in my throat.

I set the frame on my dresser, my heart aching, a mixture of longing and sorrow that I've become all too familiar with. It hangs over me like a dark cloud, never really gone, but sometimes ignorable. I do my best to ignore it now.

From down the hall, Dad calls out, "I'm gonna order pizza. That okay?"

I back away slowly, poking my head out my door. "Is it the only number you know?"

"It's the only place that delivers this late."

"Pizza it is then," I agree, rolling up my sleeves and grabbing the nearest box, looking forward to the distraction.

THE NEXT DAY COMES ENTIRELY TOO SOON. THE

metal rails of my bed shake with the force of a speeding train as a formation of jets pass overhead. The noise grows unbearably loud, crests, and then fades into the distance. Then, another wave of jets approach. The sound of freedom, my ass.

I moan, grabbing the pillow from under my head and pressing it to the upper half of my face. When the noise finally subsides, I toss the pillow aside and wrench one eye open, grasping for my cell phone. The stark white numbers confirm my feeling that it is *way* too early for that sort of thing. I open up the clock and slide the alarm off even though it isn't set to sound for fifteen more minutes.

Dawn creeps in through the slats of my cheap vinyl mini-blinds. I feel the warmth of the sun on my skin like an ant under a magnifying glass. Grudgingly, I toss the covers aside and roll my legs off the side of the bed, automatically lifting my feet as soon as they hit the cold linoleum floor. I blink, wipe my hands down my face, and sigh as I make my way upright. Hastily, I pull my violently strewn blankets into place, tossing the pillow on top, and trudge into the tiny bathroom.

The light overhead flickers on with a buzz you might expect in a hospital or a mental institution. The generic, cream-colored vanity holds a simple white basin beneath a wall-mounted mirror fastened with clear clips. The room was void of any color, except for a brown cardboard box in the corner marked "bathroom". The plain white shower liner crinkles as I sweep it aside to twist the hot water knob. While the water slowly warms to steaming hot, I take a minute to look at myself in the mirror. Pulling out the rubber band that held my chocolate-colored hair in its braid, I comb through the tangles with my fingers. Tendrils of steam curl up from the shower, causing tiny droplets of moisture to cling to my skin.

Still only half-awake, I step into the shower and let the pounding water massage the tension out of my neck and shoulders. We'd been up till the wee hours of the morning unpacking box after box of clothes, dishes, and randomness, and we still haven't made a dent. I lean against the white plastic wall and try not to hate my life.

"Be positive," my therapist always said, "and positive things will happen."

Clearly, he'd never had to share a crappy one-bathroom duplex with his dad. Still, I try to focus on the good things.

This year, there will be no one giving me dirty looks or calling me names behind my back. There will be no rotten eggs thrown at my house or dead rodents placed in my locker. There will be no long days spent in uncomfortable hospital chairs or waiting for visiting hours to begin. There will be no moping and no solitary lunches eaten in the drama room.

This year will be different.

Better.

So even if I am forced to spend the next three months in a cookie-cutter duplex in a row of cookie-cutter duplexes, in a neighborhood of... well, you get the idea, it will still be better.

Once again, a plane flies over the house with its engines at high power. The mirror in the small bathroom vibrates so hard I think it might shatter, but it holds firm.

Sighing, I rinse the frothy, apple-scented shampoo out of my hair. Today is going to be my first day of junior year. *Finally*, I think as a familiar anxious knot twists in my stomach. It's well into the first semester so the idea of slipping in unnoticed is crushed, but I'm hoping there will be so many new faces that mine won't stand out too badly. It's an on-base school, which is always nice. It's not much fun having to fight your way into cliques that formed in preschool and there's normally a pretty regular shuffle of people in and out, making it easy to get into clubs and things.

I step out of the warmth of the shower and wrap myself in a rough, olive-green towel. Military kids just seem to know what it's like to be new all the time, to have to adjust and readjust every few months. You don't get that six-month period of being a social pariah before people start talking to you. They tend to jump in with both feet. I let the thought calm my nerves as I dig through the "bathroom" box, close my hand around the handle of my blow-dryer, and pull it out.

I blow out my long, brown hair and pull it straight until it lies placidly over my shoulders. My hair is a strange combination of straight in the front and kinky in the back. I get that from my mother. If I let it do what it wanted, I'd spend my life looking like a wet poodle. Unfortunately, my hair serum, the only product under heaven that can control the frizz, is still boxed up somewhere, so I pull my hair into a high ponytail, carefully tugging the very front into a discreet, rocker chick-looking faux-hawk, and make a mental note to keep better track of my essentials next time we pack. All I've been able to find so far was my shampoo, blow-dryer, and some lip balm I'm not entirely sure is mine. I toss that back in the box, just in case.

Glancing over myself in the mirror, I wonder how much longer I can keep procrastinating. Surely, there is something else I can wash, brush, polish, or paint to keep from having to leave the small, damp room. My blue eyes look dull and milky in the yellow glow of the overhead light. I slowly rotate my face, looking for signs of an it-never-fails first-day-of-school breakout. My skin is clear, if a bit dry, with the ever present patch of freckles riding across my nose. With one dark purple fingernail, I tug at my eyes, pulling them back and wishing I had a stick of liner to apply. I sigh, giving up and pulling on my blue jeans and my favorite vintage Clash T-shirt. My favorite purple Converse low-tops are practically falling apart at the seams, but I slip my feet into them anyway and wiggle my toes experimentally. Sometimes being packed away does strange things to shoes, but these are soft with years of wear, which makes them fit perfectly to the shape of my feet.

With a final glance in my bathroom mirror, I force the remaining anxiety from my body with a hard exhale, pick up my red backpack with all its various mini-buttons from my room, and head for the kitchen and my final inspection.

DAD IS SITTING AT THE FAUX-GRANITE BREAKFAST bar, newspaper lying flat in front of him as he sips coffee from his favorite mug. The mug is a hideous greenish-brown mash-up that I'd made for him when I was in kindergarten. I'd been trying to make it look like camouflage, but it turned out more like pea soup and mud. I glance over his shoulder as I make my way past him to the pantry, dropping my bag on the counter with a clang as I go.

"The Giants looking good this season?" I ask, rummaging through the packages of instant food he picked up last night.

He grunts, his narrow eyes never leaving the paper. Must still be on his first cup, I decide.

Dad looks like your typical marine, puke-green T-shirt tucked carefully into camouflage utility pants. His hair is shaved to the skin in what they call a "high and tight," which resembles a patch of freshly mown grass on an otherwise barren lawn. His eyes are an intense blue, like mine, and his face is clean-shaven and stern. Basically, he scares the living shit out of most people, which in his chosen profession is a good thing.

After some debate, I settle on a pre-packaged snack cake and a green sports drink—the breakfast of champions.

"We need to get some real food in this place," I say, tossing the crumpled wrapper into his lap. I hop onto the counter, turn the snack cake upside down, and suck the filling through the holes in its underside.

Without looking up, he balls up the plastic and tosses it in the nearest pile of trash. "I'll do some shopping after work."

I swallow. "I could do it, if you need me to."

It's a shallow offer. I hate grocery shopping, but I'll go if it'll help him out. Another thing my therapist kept drilling into me. I have to earn Dad's trust back with small, meaningful gestures. He hasn't said anything about putting me back in therapy since the move, and I'm not sure I want to bring it up. On one hand, I can't imagine having to relive everything—again—with someone new, but on the other hand,

I can't imagine not having someone to talk to when things get bad.

And they always seem to get bad.

"Nah, that's okay, kid. I'll do it. You'd better get going, though, or you'll be late for your first day," he says, taking another sip of coffee.

Relief spreads through my body, but I just nod.

He looks up at me for the first time, his fuzzy brow furrowing in the middle. "Is that what you're wearing?"

My head jerks back. *Is he really criticizing my wardrobe?* That has to be a first. "Um, yeah. Why?"

I look down at myself, hoping I haven't forgotten anything important, like pants. To my relief, I am, indeed, fully clothed. I frown, wondering what his comment was all about. I'm covered in all the necessary places, nothing stained or torn that isn't supposed to be.

"I just thought you might want to try something less abrasive for your first day." He shifts in his seat and turns the page, turning his attention back to his paper, "You should at least try to make friends."

I'm absolutely dumbstruck by his assessment. This is abrasive? And he wants me to try to make friends? As if I hadn't tried before? "I can go put on the *Ask me about my STD* T-shirt if you prefer. It's quite a conversation starter," I quip harshly.

He sighs, and I know I'm dangerously close to upsetting him again. Dad's eyes dart to me, and then back to the paper quickly.

In fairness, there might have been some alternate-reality me who spent her days scavenging the mall for the perfect dress, getting manicures and mocking people like, well, me. But that all went out the window for me when Mom died. Now I was more of a black-or-darker girl. I've spent the last year and a half learning not to give a shit what people thought of me, and I've learned it really well.

"Lucy got here this morning. She's out front if you wanna take her today," he says.

I slide off the counter. "Really? And I can drive her?" I have to admit, I'm really surprised. I was pretty sure I wouldn't get driving privileges back until I was forty.

He nods and points to where the keys hang on a hook near the fridge.

I slurp down half my lime drink and replace the cap, stuffing the rest into my backpack for later. I've slipped some notebooks, pencils, and my tablet in my little red bag too. At my last school, there would also have been a can of pepper spray. Hopefully, I won't need that here. I do, however, tuck my wallet into my back pocket and fasten the chain onto my front belt loop. What can I say? Old habits.

"I'm taking off. You need anything?" I ask, grabbing the keys on my way out the door.

"I'm good. I'm going to be at the squadron today. Still getting pass downs from all the shops. If you need anything, call me on my cell. I don't have the office number memorized yet. I should be home around six. You alright to fend for yourself tonight?" he calls down the hall after me.

"Yeah. I'll grab something on my way home. Have fun, try not to make anyone cry," I shout through the door, shutting it behind me.

I hear him mutter right before it closes, "Right back at ya, kid."

TWO

THE ENGINE OF MY BEAUTIFUL BABY ROARS TO A stop in the student parking lot, drawing looks of admiration from the male population. Dad and I have been restoring Lucy, my gunmetal gray '67 Mustang Shelby Fastback, since I was ten. She was well worth the wait. Not that she doesn't have her little quirks, like the fact that the emergency brake is held up with safety wire, but for the most part, she's perfect. For a long time, I thought we were fixing her up for my dad, but then, for my sixteenth birthday, he'd handed me the keys and orders to Cherry Point.

I wasn't sure which I was happier about.

Looking out at the faces of strangers slowly gathering for a peek at the new girl, I take a deep breath, pat Lucy gently on the dash, and scoop my bag from the passenger seat.

With my chin held high, I step out of the car, into the harsh light of the North Carolina sun, and head for the door.

I'm still standing in line in the office when the first bell rings. There are two other new kids in front of me, an attractive senior boy transferring in from somewhere abroad, and a freshman girl from somewhere near Texas if I've heard her accent correctly. By the time the elderly secretary gets to me, first period is well underway. *Super.* Nothing says inconspicuous like bursting in during the middle of class.

Getting my schedule and map, I head off to first period. I find the correct room, do a quick double check of my schedule, and stuff the paper into my back pocket, opening the door as quietly as possible. Instantly, all eyes swing my direction. Walking in, trying my best to look more comfortable than I feel, I hand my note to the teacher, Mr. Walker.

"Class, we have a new student," he announces as my stomach sinks into my shoes. Of course he's going to be one of those teachers who makes a big deal about it. I shift my backpack onto my other shoulder and struggle to keep my chin up as he announces me. Best not to show any weakness. Teenagers, like sharks, can smell blood in the water.

"This is Farris Barnett. I trust you will all make her feel welcome."

There are a few mutterings from the back, but I can't make anything out. He makes a note on a clipboard on his desk and waves his hand in my direction.

"Why don't you tell us a little about yourself, Farris?" he says absently, lowering himself into his creaking chair.

I glance to my right, at the open windows. Maybe I can make a break for it. A fall from a second-story window couldn't possibly be more painful than this. But I'd probably end up in one of those full-body casts and be tortured by an unreachable itch for three weeks. The teacher clears his throat impatiently. Ah, the hell with it.

"Right. I'm Farris. I spend my spare time trying to calculate the air speed velocity of the European swallow. My life's ambition is to develop some sort of freeze ray, and I'm a firm believer that at some point, the world will be taken over by zombies."

Chirp, chirp, chirp. Either no one gets it, which wouldn't surprise me, or no one cares, which also wouldn't surprise me. To my left, someone snickers, but I'm too busy glancing longingly at the windows to notice who it is.

Traction is looking pretty good right now.

"Yes, well, welcome to Cherry Point High. Please take a seat in the back there." The teacher points to an empty desk in the farthest row before launching into a forty-five minute lecture on the infrastructure of post-Julius Caesar Rome. At some point, I stop taking notes on my tablet and just allow myself to zone out, scrolling through the local news instead. When the bell finally rings, I practically leap from my seat, gather my crap, and head for my next class.

I barely turn the first corner before I see it. Three tall boys, two of them in matching football jerseys and one in a black T-shirt, have another boy backed up against the lockers. They are exchanging heated words when one of them reaches out, slapping the book from the boy's hand. The hallway is filled with people, but no one is even looking at them. It's a genuine handicap, I realize. People are so willing to be blind when something like that is happening. Too often, I'd been in his shoes, tormented by others as people around me just ignored us like we were invisible. Maybe that's why I snap. Or maybe I'm just too—how did my dad put it? Abrasive.

Either way, I move in quickly, catching the tail end of the taunting.

"Why are you even here?" the tallest boy demands. "Nobody wants you here."

I pipe up. "Hey, leave him alone."

The three boys turn, looking at me as if I've just done some kind of magic trick, like pulling a rabbit out of my ass.

"What did you say?" one of them demands.

I speak very slowly. "I said, leave him alone, you giant sack of dicks."

The tall boy, he seems to be the leader of the group, shakes his head. "You're the new girl, right? This really doesn't concern you."

I cock my head to the side. "Maybe it's not my

business, but, call me crazy, I don't get the warm fuzzies when I see three people ganging up on someone."

The guy in black holds up his hands. "Hold up there, Mighty Mouse. You don't even know us. We're just chatting with our buddy, right?" He looks past me to the boy with his back against the locker. "Right?"

I turn, looking at him for the first time. His posture is stiff, but not scared. His face is stern. "It's fine."

I shrug. Hey, if he won't stand up for himself, there's not much I can do. "Fine." I look back to the others. "But you guys are still jerks."

The one in the middle chuckles. "I think you peaked with *sack of dicks*."

I flip him off because I'm pretty sure it's the international symbol for *go fuck yourself*. Bending down, I retrieve the book they knocked away and hand it to locker boy, who takes it without really looking at me, and I turn to walk away.

"Wait, new girl," one of them calls after me. I pause, turning reluctantly. The tallest of them jogs up to me, "I heard your intro in class today. Funny stuff. Any other hobbies I should know about? Besides competitive name calling?"

He smiles crookedly and flips his shaggy, blondish-brown hair out of his eyes.

He's easily six inches taller than the boys around

him, which puts him just above my eye level. I've been five foot ten since I turned fifteen and it used to bug me, but the guys are finally catching up and it's nice to be able to look them in the eyes. Especially when they're being misogynistic ass monkeys.

"I can kill a man using only a toothpick," I retort, not smiling.

The guy's lopsided grin widens. "A toothpick, huh? Sounds like quite a talent."

"It's not so much a matter of skill as one of persistence," I say with a shrug.

He laughs and steps in front of me, halting my progress. I'm about to barrel through him—and hopefully plant him square on his butt—when he does the last thing I'm expecting. He sticks out his hand.

"I'm Oliver, king of the dick sacks. It's nice to meet you, new girl."

I stare at his hand for a second like he's joking. Is he really trying to make nice after all that? I'm not sure what prompts me to take it, but it seems impossible not to. "I'm Farris. Queen of those who take no shit."

He drops my hand quickly, snatching my backpack as it slides down my arm. Slinging it over his broad shoulder, he motions for me to continue walking with a grand sweep of his arm.

"I really am sorry about that. It's personal stuff. Old drama."

I shake my head. "No excuse. And he's the one you should be apologizing to, not me."

He grins. "You're right."

My knee-jerk reaction is to wipe the smirk off his face with a well-placed kick to the nards, but I just stare at him, dumbfounded. His smile isn't mocking or arrogant; it's just sort of...sincere. I take a step forward, then another, and before I know it, we're walking together, the rest of his group peeling away in different directions.

"So, what's your next class?" he asks nonchalantly, as if we've been best friends forever. I'm so off balance that I don't quite know what to say.

Pulling my schedule out of my pocket, I read it off to him and he chuckles. "Ah, good old Mrs. Allen. You'll have to tell me what you think of her. She kinda has a polarizing effect on students. The guys love her and the girls hate her."

He shrugs off my backpack and hands it back to me. I take it, still half dazed by his behavior.

"What's that look for?" he asks.

I frown so hard my eyebrows meet in the middle of my face. "I'm trying to decide if you're going to drop a bucket of pig's blood on me or something."

He chuckles. "Not till prom, I promise."

"Well, at least you're straight about it." I hug my bag to my chest, fighting off the urge to riffle through it and make sure he hasn't lifted any of my stuff. Normally, my asshole radar is spot on, but this,

this was just downright unsettling.

"Have a good class," he says, nodding toward the door.

"Um. Yeah. Thanks," I mumble, surprised at how effectively he'd thrown me off guard.

"Let me know if you need anything. Just think of me as the unofficial welcoming committee." He tilts his head in an old-fashioned gesture and disappeared around the corner, lost to the crowd of moving students.

As I slip into a desk near the back of the room, I catch a glimpse of Mrs. Allen and immediately understand what Oliver meant. Mrs. Allen is a short woman who is so hilariously top heavy that watching her strut around the room verges on cartoonish. Her hair is long and blonde, streaked with gray, and her tight blue sweater leaves little to the imagination. To make matters worse, as she introduces herself, she leans forward, bracing herself on her desk. The front row of students, completely populated by guys, leans forward with eager smiles. Girls all over the room groan and roll their eyes. I choke back a laugh, pull out my tablet, and start taking notes, wondering in the back of my mind just what kind of person Oliver really is.

A LITTLE AFTER ELEVEN, THE BELL RINGS, AND I follow the rush of people heading to the cafeteria.

Not surprisingly, I see Oliver at a round table across the room, surrounded by a group of jocks in football jerseys and pretty girls. He doesn't seem to notice me walk in, or if he does, he's ignoring me. Either way is fine. I haven't decided yet if he falls into the maybe-friend category or the he-just-might-actually-dump-pig's-blood-on-me-at-the-prom category. I try not to notice the single dimple in his left cheek when he smiles or the way his upper lip is just a little fuller than his bottom one. As I'm busy *not* noticing these things, I trip over a backpack on the floor and am barely able to recover myself before anyone notices.

It's a much-needed wake up call.

I toss my bag down at an empty table and pull out my green sports drink. Gradually, people start coming up to me and introducing themselves. The first is a dark-haired boy and his matching girlfriend (Derek and Kayla, respectively), who remind me of an emo Barbie and Ken. He wears a long, black trench coat over dark jeans and a black leather vest. His midnight-black hair is long in the front, short in the back, a reverse mullet. Kayla is a petite thing in torn, black leggings, a red plaid skirt, and a black dress shirt, its collar held together with safety pins. Her hair is a wild mixture of magenta and electric blue, but it looks really good with her deep olive skin and makes me long for some multihued streaks of my own. The shape of her beautiful, heavily kohled gray eyes suggests she is at least part Asian.

"Nice to meet you," I offer pleasantly, glad not to be sitting alone anymore. I'd spent the bulk of my last year sitting alone in the corner of the cafeteria while the people who used to be my friends snickered and threw wrappers at me. Now here I was, feeling like a somewhat normal person again.

Weird.

"We heard you stood up to Ollie and his tribe of idiots today. That's cool," Derek offers, flicking his hair out of his eyes only to have it fall back in place again.

"Did you really call them a bag of dicks?" Kayla asks curiously.

I shake my head. "I called them a *sack* of dicks."

She laughs out loud, and it's too deep to come from that small body. "That's epic. Wish I could have seen it."

"Are they always like that?" I can't help but ask.

She says nothing but Derek answers for her. "Mostly they just leave us alone, different orbits and all that. But once in a while, yeah, they can be total dicks. Especially to Reid." He nods, and I see locker boy walking toward our table.

"Hi, I'm Reid," he says, sitting beside Kayla with his tray of pizza. He must be a friend of theirs because he immediately slides his carton of chocolate milk over to her and she accepts it without a word, plucking it open with dainty, black-polished fingernails.

"Nice to meet you," I say, offering a smile. "Officially."

"Yeah." He rakes his fingers through his messy, black hair. "About that. Thanks and all, but it's probably not a good idea to make yourself a target on their board."

I shrug and take a drink. "Your life. I just can't stand shit like that."

He nods, looking down. "Thanks, all the same. I can deal with them."

Message received. He's not interested in me sticking my nose in. "Got it. I will leave you to it then."

Another girl takes a seat, and then another. They are talking to Reid about tutoring them in chemistry, and I realize that he's not the victim I first thought. A pacifist, maybe. But not a victim. As he's talking, I see the way they hang on his words, the way they laugh just a little too loudly at his jokes. The boy has game. And why shouldn't he? He looks like a super-hot Harry Potter. He even has the glasses. Nerd chic. It's a panty dropper.

He notices me staring at him, and he blushes. It's literally so adorable that I want to fold him up in my backpack and keep him in a shoebox in my room.

And as a bonus, I realize it's day one and I'm well on my way to a full table. *Nice.*

Pushing his glasses up his thin nose, Reid blushes again.

"So, what do you think so far?" Kayla asks, twirling her multihued pigtails around her slender fingers.

"It's not bad. We're just settling in, still unpacking and stuff. I haven't really seen anything but housing and the school yet." There. Very diplomatic.

"We?" Reid asks between bites of pizza.

My stomach growls, and I realize I'm staring at his food. Not only is cafeteria pizza really good, but I haven't had real food all day and I am starving. Just looking at it makes my saliva glands hit overdrive.

"Yeah. My dad and me. He's the new CO over at VMX 195," I answer, twisting my now-empty bottle open and closed again.

Reid smiles, tears his pizza in half, and holds a piece out to me. I accept the cheesy mass without hesitation. One of the other girls asks for a bite too and Reid looks away, leaning over so she can tear a bite off with her teeth. Behind him, Oliver is staring at us with a surprised expression. When I catch his eye, he smiles a hundred-watt smile and waves like an idiot. I feel the heat hit my face before I can look away. Great, now the whole room is staring at me.

"I see Oliver has decided to fawn on you," Kayla says flatly.

I think I hear a twinge of bitterness in her voice.

She leans in close, her hair almost touching my face, and whispers, "I know Oliver is cute, but he's weird. You know, one of those charming, smart, annoyingly perfect, until-the-day-someone-finds-a-body-in-his-trunk types."

I lean back just a little and tilt my head. "Do I smell a little history there?"

She shrugs. "You could say that. His family is medical, so they've been here forever. Anyway, I remember freshman year, he took a swing at my friend Dylan for accidentally tripping him in PE." She lowers her voice. "And there were other things, too. He was always in trouble for something. It's only in the past year or so he's gone on this *being a better person* kick. Don't be fooled; it won't last for long."

I can tell by the look in her eyes that she's trying to look out for me, not something to be taken lightly, especially when you are the new kid and therefore the social outcast by default. So I give a gentle nod and munch my pizza. Reid leans back over and cuts off my view of Oliver's table.

"So what is there to do around here for fun? Clubbing baby seals? Sketchy college raves? Ooh, what about the ever-classic underground hobo fights?" I ask.

"Well, if you'd like, we could take you down to the Circle tonight," Reid offers, then he pauses and gestures to Derek. "We're all going. We could show you around the boardwalk and stuff, if you're interested."

I glance over at Derek and Kayla, but they're busy. Each has inserted a speaker bud in one ear and begun playing some game on Kayla's phone that requires vigorous shaking and laughing.

"I'd like to, but I still have to unpack and stuff." I frown. A night out sounds really good, but did I dare ask Dad to go out on a school night? So soon?

Besides, I've actually been looking forward to unpacking, then snuggling up with a book, but I can't stay inside hiding out forever. *Why not give it a go?* a small voice inside me whispers. It's the *before* voice. The one I used to listen to. Since Mom died, I'd mostly listened to my *after* voice. The one that said, *Stay in. Hide out. Be safe.*

I sit up straight, squaring my shoulders. "How 'bout Friday night?" I offer, stuffing the last bite of pizza in my mouth.

Reid's head snaps up, his eyes searching my face for a moment before answering. "Sure. Friday then," he says smoothly, a goofy grin on his square face.

Kayla nudges Derek and packs away her phone just as the first bell rings.

"Nice to meet you, Farris. See you around, Reid," Derek offers with a grand bow before putting his arm around Kayla and walking away.

She gives me a wave as they march their way past a group of kids sitting by the doors, who gawk after the duo. I have to admit, as a couple, they *are* stare worthy.

"You know, my parents are in your dad's squadron," Reid says as he dumps his tray in the trash, stacking it in the tray-return window.

"Both of them?" I ask, surprised.

It's rare for a kid to have both parents in the service, much more rare to have them in the same squadron. Actually, it's kind of a big no-no as I understand.

He nods. "They're two of the best pilots in the fleet, so they both got selected for the JSF."

The Joint Strike Fighter was the newest addition to the Marine Corps Air Wing. VMX 195 would be the first fully operational Joint Strike Fighter squadron in the military. My dad was sent here to oversee the squadron and its operations. It's kind of a big deal, at least to him.

"That's cool," is what I say, but *that's terrifying* is the thought running through my head.

Every military brat knows the risk of losing a parent in the line of duty is high, especially now, but to have both parents in the line of fire is truly a frightening thought. Of course, with my mom gone, I suppose I am sort of in the same boat. If I lost Dad, I'd be all alone. I quickly push the thought away.

"They must be gone a lot. Where do you get shipped off to?" I ask, mildly curious.

He frowns. "Technically, I'm supposed to be with my uncle in Cleveland, but they don't like to pull me out of school—especially for the stupid two-week training detachments and stuff. So I usually just stay here."

"Alone?" I can't keep the envy from my voice. "Lucky."

He grins. "I can take care of myself. I mean, even when they are here, they're too busy to really be *here,* you know?"

The sad thing is, I do understand. This year is going to be that way for me, too. Dad will be working all hours and gone on all the detachments.

"Maybe I can hammer out a similar arrangement with my dad. Anything beats staying at my aunt's old-folks' home."

"And we could keep each other company," he offers with a grin. "We could alternate throwing raging parties and hosting underground hobo fights."

I frown. "Somehow, I think I would have to agree to one of those ankle monitors parolees get. My dad is a tad overprotective."

"Good. That means he cares."

"Yeah, it's great until he takes away my shoelaces and makes me start using those little safety scissors."

Reid laughs, leading the way through the maze of people rushing through the doors and back into the hallway. The first bell rings, causing a chorus of slamming lockers and rushed goodbyes as everyone heads back to class. I pull out the wrinkled map and schedule from my pocket, staring at the complicated maze of stairs and rooms, searching for my next class.

"Here." Reid holds out his hand for the schedule.

I hand it over. He quickly scans it before pointing to the nearest stairwell.

"Up the stairs, third door on the left. Or you could just walk with me. That's my next class, too."

He sounds happy about that. I have to admit, I'm kind of happy about it, too. It'll be nice to have someone to talk to. We stop at the bottom of the stairs so I can grab a drink at the water fountain when Oliver and his lemmings come up behind us.

"Hey, new girl, you finding your way around all right?" Oliver asks, his tone playful.

I wipe my mouth on my sleeve and turn to see Reid standing still as a statue between the herd of guys and me. Oliver straightens up as I turn; apparently, he'd been leaning over me. None of Oliver's group seems aggressive or bullish, but they are defiantly... imposing. Plus, I still don't like the way Reid reacts to them. He's so tense he's practically vibrating.

"Yeah, I'm fine, just heading to chemistry with my new friend, Reid," I answer, plastering a smile on my face.

The boys look back at Reid as if noticing him for the first time. He keeps his head up, knees locked. Oliver's smile falters for just a second as he looks at the skinny boy. "Hey, sorry about earlier."

He sounds sincere enough, but Reid ignores him, making me wonder if it's all just a show for my benefit. Finally, he turns his attention back to me.

"Chem is my next class, too. You guys mind if I walk with you?"

Without waiting for a response, he grabs my backpack from my hands and tosses the football he's been carrying to one of his buddies as he takes the first step up the stairs. I reach over, meaning to put my hand on Reid's shoulder to make sure he is all right, but before I can touch him, he mutters a "see you later" and bolts up the stairs in front of us. I stand there, unsure what to do. He's obviously skittish around Oliver, and some nagging, nosy part of me wants to know why.

Oliver smiles sheepishly. "Relax, new girl, I don't bite. I just wanted a chance to get to know you a little better. He kind of monopolized you at lunch."

I open my mouth to protest, but no words come out. For the second time in one day, he has me all twisted up in the head. Finally, I figure there's only one way to know for sure, and that's to get to know him. Cautiously.

I drop in beside him, and we walk to class together. I'm overly careful not to graze his arm with my own as we move.

He runs his fingers through his hair, looking a little nervous as we approach the door. Stopping short, he looks at me. "I was just wondering if you're busy tonight. Maybe I could take you to a movie or something?"

His eyes are sky-blue, I notice, and hopeful, stunningly so. For a second, I forget how to talk. What the actual fuck is wrong with me today?

"I actually have to unpack tonight. Our house is still all boxed up, so—"

He doesn't even let me finish. "Perfect. I'll come by at about five. We can hang out and I'll help you unpack. Do you like Chinese?"

My brain sputters like a car backfiring. What is he thinking? My back stiffens. I'm about to tell him no when something stops me. It's the dimple that finally does me in. I never thought I'd find myself quite so... I don't even know if I'm intrigued or just stupefied. But that dimple is magical. It clearly has the ability to make smart girls do stupid things.

Besides, I tell myself, the idea has merit. If he tries anything, I can slap a jerk label on him and send him packing. If not, well, that has possibilities, too.

I shake my head. "Yeah. Sure. I guess."

"Great. I'll bring the takeout."

"And I'll bring the pepper spray, so don't even think of trying anything," I add quickly.

Bowing his head, he hands me my bag. "Wouldn't dream of it."

He gives me a quick wave as he takes off for his seat at the back of the room. I shake my head again, as if to clear away the last of the shock. I'll give Oliver this much, he's certainly unexpected.

Navigating the rows of desks, I slide into an empty seat beside Reid, who slumps forward, one arm folded under his chin, doodling on the cover of his notebook.

"Hey, I thought you were going to walk me to class?" I ask playfully, trying to break the tension.

The bell rings.

"It looked like you had a better offer," he whispers, shooting a dirty look over his shoulder to where Oliver sits.

I sit back, unsure what to say, but my curiosity grows by the minute.

Must be a testosterone thing.

THREE

T WO MORE CLASSES AND THE DAY IS FINALLY OVER. A few people initiate the usual curious-about-the-new-kid conversations. You know, where are you from, what bases have you lived at, what brings you here, the old standby stuff people ask when they want to be polite but don't really want to get to know you. I try to be gracious, I really do, but all I want to do is stab myself in the eye with a fork.

I used to be a people person, I really did.

Once upon a time in another life.

I walk to my car, my bag heavy with the new textbooks I've been assigned. To my surprise, Reid is waiting for me. He hadn't spoken a word during chemistry and vanished as soon as the bell rang. I didn't see him the rest of the day, but I'm glad he's here.

He leans against my passenger door, his glasses reflecting the late-day sun.

"Hey," I say gently.

"Hey. Look, I want to apologize for earlier. It's

just that Oliver and I, well, we don't really get along."

I snicker. "Noticed. I assume there's a story behind that."

He looks away. "Yeah, but if it's all the same, I don't really want to tell it. Let's just say we were friends once, and then we weren't. No one can push your buttons like people you used to be close to."

I nod, knowing that all too well. Being close to someone is basically like handing them a knife and turning your back. Eventually, they will stab you in it.

"I get that." I bite my bottom lip. "And it's clearly none of my business."

He looks back at me and smiles. "Cool."

A weaker girl would have meddled. But I resist. Barely.

"Do you need a ride home or something?" I ask, scanning the parking lot. I don't want to be rude, but he's still leaning on my car.

He stands up and takes a step back, pointing to a baby-blue scooter. "Nah, see that sleek man-machine? That's me."

I choke back a giggle. "Ah, yes. It's very manly," I joke, hoping he isn't the kind of guy who gets super sensitive about his ride.

"It's okay, you can laugh. I'm saving up for a Ninja, so..."

"That's funny, I'm saving up for a pirate," I retort.

He snickers. "Cute and quick with the lame

jokes, we might just have to be friends, Farris."

I hold up a finger. "On one condition. Tell me how you feel about Captain Jack Harkness."

He puckers his lips, looking very serious. "He makes me question my own sexuality."

I smile. Oh yes, we're going to be great friends. We might even need some kind of secret handshake.

"And as for the scooter, I needed something to get me around town once I had my license. With my parents' schedules, I used to have to walk to my karate classes. At least now I can ride in semi-comical style."

"Karate class? For real?"

He shrugs. "I was a hyper kid; the parents thought it might help me channel some energy."

"Yeah, nothing says calm down like learning to face-kick people." I pause. "Don't you find it a tad ironic that you want to drive a Ninja to karate class?"

"Oh my God." He laughs. "I'd never thought of it like that. Yes, I guess it is."

As we are talking, a girl approaches. She's one of the blondes that sat with us at lunch, but they look so similar I have a hard time remembering her name. Bethany? Stephanie? Luckily, Reid turns.

"Hey, Cassy."

"Hey Reid, um..." She looks at me, snapping her fingers like she's trying to remember my name too. Good. I don't feel bad anymore.

"Farris," I help her out.

"Right." She looks back at Reid. "So, can I talk to you for a sec?"

Not wanting to get in the way of Reid and his fan club, I give him a wave and toss my bag across the seat before sliding in and bringing Lucy roaring to life. I watch as they walk away. She throws her arms around his neck in a flirty hug before bouncing off, leaving him to mount his scooter.

As I pull out of the student lot, I catch sight of Oliver sprinting across the football field with the other jocks in uniform. I have to admit, it's kind of hot. Must be some primal part of my brain recognizing the potential hunter-gatherer alpha-male thing. I shake my head at the thought. That Psych class is really going to mess with me, I can tell.

As it turns out, the hardest part of my day is finding my house.

Every corner looks the same; there are no landmarks and all the streets are named after lame things like flowers or fruit. It takes me half an hour of wandering around the base to get home. When I get inside, I feel my phone vibrate in my pocket and pull it out. It's a text from Dad.

Hey, kid. Gonna be here a little later than I thought. Unpack what you can without me, but leave the heavy stuff. I'll try to get out of here around seven. I'll get myself some food at the chow hall so go ahead and eat without me. See you later. D.

Dinner. It's only four o'clock, but I'm ravenous

from missing lunch. I stand at the counter, balancing on one foot and debating whether to pop in a pizza or just grab a snack.

I can't help but wonder if my mysterious football player will actually show. Come to think of it, I never told him where I lived. I smack myself on the forehead. It was so *me* to meet a cute guy, make plans, and then forget to tell him where to meet me or give him my number. I take out a small bag of trail mix and settle in at the kitchen table to do my homework.

The next time I look up, the microwave is blinking 4:50 and I realize I'm still hungry. Doubtful there is any way Oliver is going to locate me in this tangled mess of base housing, I decide it's time to eat.

I've just begun foraging for something when my doorbell rings. The tone is just unfamiliar enough that it throws me for a second. I glance out the window and standing there, on my porch, is Oliver. He's in a fresh black-collared shirt and jeans, holding a bag from a place called Chopstix. I smooth my hair and T-shirt, then open the door. His smile is part boyish and sweet, part rugged and mysterious.

The perfect combination for getting me into trouble.

"Hi!" I say, still surprised. "I didn't think you'd be able to find me." I open the door and he steps in, handing me the white plastic sack.

"Well, I'm full of surprises." He winks and walks past me into the kitchen, stepping over boxes and mounds of paper as he goes.

That is an understatement.

He hops onto the counter. "Plus, it's a small base. Not hard to find the only '67 Shelby in a hundred miles." He waves his hand around. "I thought your dad was an officer. How come you guys landed in enlisted housing?"

Setting the bag beside him, I pull out the takeout boxes, inspecting each one. I can tell by the smell that the first one is Kung Pao Chicken, and therefore mine. As soon as I open it, my stomach clenches with hunger.

"They're backlogged with the construction. It's not so bad here, though. Except for the one-bathroom thing." I frown, pluck some chopsticks out of the bag, and hop up beside him, handing him the other box of food. I'm not sure, but it smells like Moo shu pork.

"Thanks," he says, taking it without complaint. "Yeah, I don't get the bathroom thing. Why do girls need their own bathrooms, anyway? Do you do some super-secret lady stuff in there?" He rolls his chopsticks together, and then maneuvers them expertly into his hand, taking a big mouthful.

"Yeah. Top secret. I can't even hint at it or I'll have my chick license revoked. That and I hate smelling like my dad's Old Spice body wash after I shower." I shudder in mock horror.

He leans over to me and takes a long whiff.

No lie.

He *sniffs* me.

"You smell pretty good to me."

I blush before I can stop myself, the heat licking up my neck and face. *Down girl*, I scold myself. This is so not the way *after Farris* behaved. *After Farris* is made of sterner stuff.

I roll my eyes and take a bite, trying to regain my cool. The food is really good. Spicy, but not my-friggin'-mouth-is-on-fire hot.

"Thanks for dinner. No offense, but why do you want to spend your evening helping me unpack?" I ask after I swallow and take a sip of soda. "I'm sure you've got better things to do."

Everything about his behavior has my suspicious side on full alert, but his voice and body language put me at ease. He has the charisma of a southern gentleman, with eyes that practically dance with mischief.

He takes a breath, sticking his chopsticks in the box. "Honestly, I'm not sure. I'm trying to figure you out, I suppose."

I feel myself make a face. "What do you mean?"

He shrugs. "I dunno. I don't think I've ever seen anyone stand up for a stranger the way you did today. It's odd..."

I raise one eyebrow, "You think I'm odd?"

He shifts. "No, not like that. But you just kind of, I dunno. I don't know how to make it make sense. I just saw you and knew I wanted to know you better."

I take another bite. "So this is a science experiment? Did you bring the chloroform? Because it's not a party till someone brings the chloroform."

"See, that's why I wanted to get to know you better. You're sharper than most girls I know. Quick and smart. And you clearly aren't afraid of anything. So why haven't you told me to get lost yet?" he asks with a smile.

"I don't know. You kind of intrigue me too, I guess. You never do or say what I expect you to. It's kind of annoying," I point out.

"Fair enough." He chuckles. "But kind of charming, too, right?"

I raise my eyebrow again. "I'm gonna stick with annoying. But we'll see how the night goes."

He clutches his hand to his heart, pretending to be wounded. I smile and nudge him with my elbow. I don't even think about it, but the moment it happens, something curls into a ball in my stomach. It feels easy. Warm.

"So, are you going to put me to work or what?" he asks as I scrape the bottom of my mostly empty takeout box.

"I warn you, I am a bit of a slave driver," I joke, getting down from the counter and tossing my empty container back into the bag.

His eyes sparkle impishly. "I hoped as much."

I pick up a small box of books and heave it into his lap. "These go on the shelf in the living room."

He grunts dramatically as he carries the heavy box into the other room. I grab a box of my own and follow him.

"Wow, you have quite the library," he says as we shelve the two boxes.

"These are just my hardcovers. The paperbacks are in my room," I mutter, checking the title in my hand to make sure I put it in its proper place in the series order. I stuff it in its spot between two others.

"So obviously you like to read..." he prompts, leaning back on his palms.

"Yep," I say, picking up the next book. Actually, that is a severe understatement. I devour books like a fat kid devours cake.

"What do you like?" he volleys back.

I pause, and then slide the book into its spot. "Um, a little of everything. Except true crime."

"Why not true crime?"

I stop and look at him, half laughing. "Why?"

He leans forward. "Well, we're sitting here talking, or I'm talking, and you aren't saying anything."

I bristle. "Maybe I'm not a chatterbox, but I thought I was holding up my part of the conversation."

He shakes his head. "No. I mean you aren't saying anything important. Tell me something."

"What? Like the human head weighs eight pounds?"

"No. Something about you. Tell me something about yourself that you aren't sure you want me to know."

I take a deep breath. "I'm really not that interesting."

He smiles, leaning forward and plucking the book out of my hands. "I find you very interesting, but don't avoid the question."

"You didn't ask me a question," I respond, laughing again, this time uncomfortably.

He stares at me. "All right, what's your *least* favorite movie of all time?"

"That's an odd question. Okay. My *least* favorite movie is *Legends of the Fall*," I answer, taking the book back from him and searching for its place on the shelf.

"Why?" he asks, looking surprised. "I thought chicks loved Brad Pitt movies."

I shrug, turning back to him only after I've shelved my book. He's looking at me expectantly. "I suppose because everyone is so miserable all the time, like they just can't catch a break in life. Every second of their lives is hard and sad and they never get to be with the people they love."

"So watching them struggle and hurt makes you hurt, too?" he asks quietly.

I hadn't thought of it that way. "I guess. Are you

taking psychology, too?" I try to joke, but I can't make the smile reach my eyes so I look away.

"So you live here with your dad? Where's your mom? Divorced?"

The question startles me. I don't know why, it's a perfectly normal question. I guess it's just still hard to talk about, especially with a total stranger. When I answer, my voice is barely a whisper. "Dead."

"Oh, I'm sorry."

I shrug. I hear him move behind me and for a minute, I'm afraid he's going to try to hug me or something. Hearing stuff like that can make people react in off ways. They want to comfort you, but they aren't really sure how. As I brace for his touch, I hear him tear open another box. He chuckles, and I glance over my shoulder to see what's so funny. Oliver clutches a small, purple picture frame to his chest.

"What's that?" I ask, trying to remember what picture might be in that frame.

"You know, I never would have pegged you for a cheerleader." He snickers.

My face drops instantly. Lurching backward, I try to grab the frame from him, but he leans away, just out of my reach.

"I wasn't a cheerleader," I say petulantly. "It was freshman year, and it was the pom squad." Even to me, that excuse sounds lame. A sweater monkey is a sweater monkey.

He holds the picture out to me, and then snatches it back as I reach for it. "I think you look cute," he taunts, his voice raising an octave on the word *cute*.

I give him my best glare. "Look, if you value your life, you will hand me that photo right now and never speak of this again." I hold my hand out and wait.

"I don't see what the big deal is," he says, handing me the frame. "It's nothing to be ashamed of. Lots of my friends are cheerleaders."

I run my thumb over the picture. It's an odd feeling, like looking at a stranger inside your skin. I don't know that girl anymore. It was the smiling face of *before* Farris. Before my boyfriend dumped me. Before Mom got sick. Before all my friends turned against me.

"I wasn't always like this, you know," I whisper. "I used to be fun. Normal." *Happy*, I add silently.

Oliver scoots closer until his shoulder touches mine as we sit side by side.

"Oh, I think you're fun. And as for normal, well, normal is overrated." He smiles and it's like the sun peeking through the clouds, brightening everything. "You wanna tell me what happened?"

"You wondered why I stepped in like that today, when you were giving Reid a hard time. It's because I've been in that spot. Back against the wall while everyone tells you how worthless you are and how much they wish you were gone. Only no one stepped up for me." I shake my head, trying to shake away the memories. "It does things to you. Inside."

I lay the picture on the floor facedown and hand him another box. "And that's as much as you're going to hear about it."

With a single nod, he takes the box, pulling it open. "Looks like speakers and cables in this one," he says, changing the subject like a pro.

"Just sit that one in the corner."

He obeys, opening the next box. It's a pile of old circuit boards, hard drives, and wires.

"What's all this? You building a rocket or something?"

I take the box, setting it in my lap. "Sort of. I like building computers."

He does a quick double take. "Like, you *build* computers?"

I raise one shoulder to my chin. "See, I'm a wealth of surprises myself."

"I'm seeing that. It's an odd hobby; how'd you pick it up?"

I rummage through the box as I answer. "Mom was an artist. She could paint, make pottery, stuff like that. Me... not so much. But computers, coding, switches, and circuits? It's music to me. It just makes sense inside my head. I can look at a string of code, tell you exactly what it's supposed to do, and how elegantly it's designed. It's my art."

He whistles. "That's impressive. So do you have a cool hacker name?"

I roll my eyes. "I'm not one of those. Hacking, it's all about the ego. It's like breaking something just to prove you can. Not really my style. I like creating. Games mostly. I designed a *Battlestar Galactica* game that would knock your socks off." I pause. "You know, if you were into gaming."

"I game," he says, looking affronted.

"Cool, what do you play?" I realize once the words are out that they sound like a challenge, which I don't mean to do at all.

He squirms. "I like Monopoly. And Clue. And Risk. And I play *Call of Duty* on the PS3 sometimes."

I lower my chin, smiling. "That's cool. I like tabletop games too."

He relaxes back, as if he'd been nervous. Good, let me make him nervous for once.

An hour, three root beers, and a lengthy discussion about the sexist treatment of females on *Battlestar Galactica* later, I hear my dad's car in the driveway. My first thought is, *Oh shit!* But I'm sixteen and it's not like we're doing anything wrong. Still, deep down, I worry about Dad's reaction.

The door swings open with more drama than is really necessary and my dad, all six feet, six inches of him, trudges through the door. Oliver seems perfectly at ease, despite the entrance.

"Hi, Dad!" I greet him with just a little too much

enthusiasm.

If he's upset, it doesn't show. His face is calm, unreadable, except for the subtle raising of one eyebrow. No one but me would've even noticed it, I'm sure.

"Hey there, kid. Who's your friend?" he asks.

I realize in that moment I have no idea what Oliver's last name is, and I don't think king of the dick sacks is going to cut it. "Oh! Dad, this is Oliver. Oliver, this is my dad, Lieutenant Colonel Barnett."

"'Sir' is fine," Dad corrects me.

Oliver stands like he's been training for this moment all his life, the Parent Olympics, and holds his hand out to my father. "Oliver Knight, sir. Nice to meet you."

I let out a nervous breath. The boy has skills.

Dad shakes his hand, then looks around at the scattered empty boxes and mess. "I see my daughter's put you to work, but it's getting late, so..."

Oliver nods. "Yes, sir, I should get going." He looks at me. "I'll see you tomorrow."

I walk him to the door as Dad crosses into the kitchen. "Sure. And Oliver, thanks for the food and the company. It was nice."

"Call me Ollie. All my friends do." He smiles. "And anytime."

Oliver pauses on the step for a minute, looking like he wants to say something else, but changes his mind and walks over to his orange Dodge Dakota pickup truck. I close the door against the sight of his taillights and proceed into the kitchen where Dad is no doubt waiting to ambush me.

He sits at the table, rummaging through the open box of framed pictures. I've been saving the wall stuff for last. Base housing frowns upon things like nail holes in the walls, so I wanted to get Dad's okay before I hung anything. He plucks out a picture of Mom and me a few months before she died. The cancer had already taken her hair by then, but she was still the most beautiful woman I've ever known. She was sitting on the edge of our gray sofa, a bright yellow scarf wrapped around her head. I was sitting half in her lap as she played with my hair. We were both laughing. She did that a lot, right up until the end. Even when the meds had taken everything else, her smile still shined like the sun. A lump forms in my throat, and I have to swallow it down. There's no crying. It's an unspoken agreement between us. We don't cry, because once we start, we might never stop.

I take a deep breath and come up behind Dad, hugging his shoulders. He pats my hands twice and pulls away.

"So, first day and the boys are already following you home, huh?" he asks, slipping the photo back into the box. I reach into it behind him and pull the picture out, walking it over to the bookshelf in the living room and setting it carefully on the top shelf.

I graze my hand over Mom's face once before going back into the kitchen.

"Yeah, that's me. I'm like the Pied Piper of Cherry Point. You're gonna have to beat them off with a stick," I say flatly.

He doesn't think it's funny, based on the expression on his face. It looks more like he's just taken a big bite of something sour.

"Sit down, Farris." He pushes a chair out with his foot.

Crap. He never calls me by my name; it's always kid, unless I'm in trouble. This could be ugly.

Sitting down, I fold my right leg under me. I haven't found the seat cushions that belong to these chairs yet, and they are pretty darn uncomfortable without them. "Yeah, Dad?"

I hold my breath. How bad could it be? It's not like he caught me making out with Oliver or anything. *And if he had?* part of my brain thinks defiantly. I silence the small voice as quickly as it comes.

"I know you're sixteen, and I know you're developing feelings—" He screws up his face. "And...I wish your mother were here," he says, pinching his nose with his thumb and forefinger, closing his eyes.

"Whoa. Time-out." I signal it with my hands. "Let me just stop you right there. This is quickly turning into a bad after-school special, so I'll just say this. Please, please don't lecture me about being responsible or anything like that. I know how badly I've screwed up in the past, but I'm working really hard to get myself together again. And I promise, I have no intention of doing anything stupid."

He is quiet for a minute. "I know all that, honey. I want to trust you. I want you to go out, have fun, and just be a teenager. I know that every once in a while, you'll break curfew, get into trouble—not *big* trouble—and just be a normal kid. And what happened..." He trails off.

What can he say? That it wasn't my fault? Because it totally was and we both know it.

When he speaks again, his voice is tentative. "I'm afraid sometimes that you've had to grow up too fast, losing your mom the way you did. I don't want you to miss out on anything."

I have to catch myself before the wave of disgust I'm feeling registers on my face. Even my dad wants me to just be normal. Well, I'm here, aren't I? I'm trying.

Maybe I'm not normal. Maybe I never will be again. But maybe, just maybe, I can fake it.

The months I'd spent taking care of Mom had given me reason to grow up fast. Every night, for 392 nights, I went to bed wondering if I'd have a mother when I woke up. I held wet washcloths to her head when she threw up, and at the end, I changed bandages, took temperatures, and fought to keep a smile on my face for her. Inside, I was dying just as much as she was. I was probably the most responsible fourteen-year-old on the planet. That's why it was such a shock when I blew up. I'd been wound so tightly for so long, I figured I needed a break. And, boy, did I get one.

And it had cost me everything.

"Okay, Dad. I'll start this weekend. I got invited to go out with some kids Friday night. I promise to be a good twenty minutes late getting home."

He smiles half-heartedly. "Deal. And as for this Oliver boy... keep an eye on him. He reminds me of myself at that age."

I scrunch up my face. That is just *disturbing*.

FOUR

IT'S WELL PAST MIDNIGHT WHEN MY HEAD FINALLY hits the pillow. Almost all the boxes are empty, broken down into neat, flat stacks and stored in the empty utility room. We don't own a washer or dryer since officer housing usually comes with them, so I'll be making a laundry run on Saturday. I fall asleep quickly, dreaming of spinning washer drums and dark, perilous water.

The next two days, Oliver is conspicuously absent from school. I try to ignore it, the urge to look for his face in the crowded halls or the need to glance over to his lunch table, just in case. But there's no denying it, so I settle for at least trying not to be too obvious. The week passes in a haze of memorizing classrooms, connecting names with faces, and mastering my elusive locker combination. My little lunchtime table group becomes customary, and I quickly find myself falling into a comfortable groove. After a few days, I forget to look for Oliver, or at least that's what I tell myself. When Reid catches me looking over my shoulder at lunch Thursday, he waves his hand in front of my face.

"These are not the droids you're looking for," he says playfully.

I let my face fall, my voice going completely monotone. "These aren't the droids we're looking for."

Then I blink, as if pulling myself from a daze. He chuckles. "Wow, I didn't think that would work."

I smirk and shrug one shoulder. "The force is strong with you."

As it turns out, Reid and I share not only a borderline-idiotic sense of humor, but also a disturbing ability to converse in *Star Wars* quotes—a talent we abuse for the remainder of lunch. Bianca and Cassy, both bottle blondes dressed in tight Gap jeans, look genuinely put out as they try to keep up with the nearly unstoppable flow of randomness spewing from our mouths. Derek grins every so often, catching a speeding reference, but doesn't join in. Cassy's face is soft, the kind of plumpness you see on babies and cherubic Michelangelo paintings. Her lashes are dark and thick and her skin is creamy white with a flush of natural pink on her round cheekbones. She's really pretty, I realize. And she keeps glancing up at Reid like...

Something clicks into place in my brain. She likes him. Of course she does. It's on the way her chin is always tilted toward him just a fraction, the way she touches him casually, even in the way she tucks a strand of blonde waves behind her ear when he looks at her. I swing my gaze to Bianca. She's thinner, her face more angular and tight. She's holding herself more stiffly, her arms folded across her chest, legs crossed away from them. Either she's not interested, or she's painfully shy. It could really go either way. I take the opportunity to bring them into the conversation.

"Have you ever seen *Star Wars*?" I ask in Cassy's direction. She fidgets with her tiny silver cross necklace as Reid turns his attention to her. She blushes just a little.

"Oh, no. I don't think so. I'd like too though. It sounds really good."

"I've only seen the new ones," Bianca admits, drawing a gasp and over-exaggerated chest clutch from both Reid and myself.

"You need to see it," Reid says, and I nod.

Cassy looks down, one hand combing through her loose hair. She opens her mouth to say something else, but she's cut off by the shrill ringing of the bell. Grabbing my tray, I follow Bianca to the trash, leaving Reid and Cassy to finish their conversation, but when I turn around, Reid is right behind me and Cassy is halfway out the door. I feel genuinely bad. I know all too well what it's like to be excluded. In the back of my mind, I make a note to try to keep her in the conversation next time.

That afternoon, we all hang out in the parking lot after school. Cassy manages to secure an invite to go watch movies at Reid's house that weekend, and I'm invited too. I watch her expression fall a little at the change of course.

"I dunno. I'm on laundry mat duty this weekend," I say honestly. The conversation drifts again, and we all split up before Reid finally hops on his scooter and putters away.

As social lives go, I've had worse.

My alarm goes off Friday morning about three hours too early for my liking. When I finally drag myself into the dull, off-white kitchen for breakfast, Dad is facedown into his laptop, clicking away furiously. I sit down beside him, my Tasty Os nearly overflowing their green ceramic bowl. Dad slides a fifty across the table to me without looking up.

"What's this for? You need to put a hit out on someone?" I ask, my mouth full of cereal.

"Sweetheart, if you're only getting fifty bucks for a contract kill, you need to up your rates."

"I'll take that under advisement," I say through another bite.

He snickers. "It's lunch money, oh daughter of mine. Begging for money is a time-honored teenage tradition. By never participating, you're throwing the whole cosmic system out of balance."

I nod and stuff the bill in my wallet. And to think I just got used to prepackaged pastries and sports drinks, too.

A few more minutes of clicking and I've had it. Dad is great at many things, but computers are not on that list. He's about as gentle as a bull in a china shop, and I can practically hear the poor keyboard crying for help.

"Dad, is everything ok? Do you need something?"

He sits up, sighing heavily. "Can you do that thing?"

I blink.

He waves his hand, sliding the computer across the table to me. "That thing where I can wirelessly connect to my desktop from this?"

I laugh, taking the computer, "You got the IP address of the other computer?"

He nods, sliding a scrap of paper my way.

Opening his system files, I begin rooting around. "You know, there are people who get paid for this kind of thing," I say.

Dad stands up, shrugging into his camouflage jacket. "What's your point?" he asks.

I bite my lip. "Well, in the spirit of teenage begging, I was hoping you'd let me use the credit card to pick up a few new things for my room."

He frowns, his eyebrows knitting together in the center of his face. "What's wrong with the stuff you have?"

I shake my head. "Well, first off, there's no overhead lighting, so I need a few lamps. Also, my old curtains aren't the right size for the new window. Plus, I've had that same comforter since I was nine. Pink flowers aren't really my thing anymore."

Reluctantly, he pulls out his tattered brown wallet and flips the silver Visa card onto the table. "Okay. Just try to keep it reasonable, huh? And why don't you swing by the squadron today and I'll give you a tour?"

I wink and stuff it in my pocket behind the cash with one hand, still typing with the other. "Here," I say, sliding the computer back to him. "All fixed."

He leans over and kisses the top of my head. "What would I do without you?"

"Work from your desktop like a caveman?" I grin.

I GET AN EARLY TEXT FROM KAYLA ASKING FOR A RIDE to school, so I clean up quickly and head to her house. It's a row of enlisted housing not far from my own, only the duplexes are a pale rose color rather than tan and her house has huge eggplants growing in the three-foot square patch of dirt under the living room window. Derek and Kayla sit on the narrow stoop, their heads so close together that at first I think they're kissing. Then Kayla leans back, tilting her chin skyward. I roll down my window and shout to them.

"Hey guys, you ready?"

Derek is wearing black denim jeans, a sliced-up grey T-shirt, and a leather dog collar with silver spikes. It's a conservative look compared to what he normally wears. His jet-black hair is stretched together at the crown of his head in a faux-hawk, his eyeliner thick and perfect around his caramel-brown eyes. I try really hard not to envy his long lashes and high cheekbones. Had Derek been born a girl, he would have put me to shame.

"Hop in," I offer, turning down the stereo, the only non-authentic component in the entire car.

Derek slides in the passenger side and Kayla climbs over him, maneuvering her petite little body to sit on the console between us, her red-and-black plaid skirt bunching under her. I don't know what kind of perfume she's wearing, but it immediately fills the cramped car with the scent of lavender—not real lavender, but the kind they use to artificially scent cleaning products. It burns my nostrils.

"What's going on?" I ask, leaving my window down, hoping to dissipate the odor as we drive.

Kayla flips her hair over her shoulder. Today, it's separated into hundreds of delicate braids, each with a multicolored rubber band at the bottom.

"Nothing. Just hanging out," she answers, turning the music back up. "Derek likes to get out of the house before his stepdad wakes up and starts giving him shit about his ensemble."

Derek turns his head, looking out the window as we pull into the parking lot. "Yeah," he says simply.

Not sure what to say to that, I reach out and touch one of Kayla's earrings. It's a tiny guitar pick with a hole drilled through the tip.

"Nice," I offer.

"Thanks. I got it in Raleigh." She fiddles with her tall, black boots. "We should go up there and go shopping. I know where all the good places are."

"Sure. That'd be cool," I say, thinking it over. I imagine myself stepping out of my room in an outfit like hers. Then I imagine my dad clutching his chest as the heart attack drops him to his knees.

"Kayla lives down the street from me, so we walk together," Derek says as he slips on a pair of dark sunglasses with silver skulls on the sides. "But today..." He trails off, pointing to her boots. I raise one eyebrow, not needing further explanation.

"Yeah. We can't all have fancy cars to tool around in. But it would be handy," Kayla says, running her hand across the dashboard like she's petting a dog. "She's so pretty."

I pat the dash proudly. "This car was just a hunk of scrap metal when Dad brought her home. It took us years to rebuild her, piece by piece."

Rebuilding this car had been one of the only things that kept Dad sane while Mom was getting sicker and sicker. When he was working in the garage, he didn't have to think about anything else. For a long time, I resented that, the time it took away from Mom. Then he started letting me help, and it sort of brought us together. No, Lucy was much more than a car, fabulous though she was.

Kayla looks me in the eye, cocking her head to the side. It's like she's reading my mind, or maybe just my expression. It makes my back stiffen and my muscles tense.

"Fair enough," she says finally, not pressing for more details. "So, about that shopping trip..."

The rigidity eases out of my body. Kayla picks at her chipped, black nail polish while describing the city layout. I'm only half-listening. A familiar truck pulls into the lot, distracting me.

Oliver parks a few rows in front and to the left of me. After not seeing him for days, the sight of him makes my breath catch in my lungs. Trying to be subtle, I watch from the corner of my eye as he jumps out of his truck, slinging his dark blue backpack over one shoulder. He isn't wearing a football jersey today; rather, he's looking super formal in tan slacks and a white shirt with a blue tie. He was cute the last time I saw him; today, he's downright sexy.

"They make the players wear dress clothes on game day," Kayla says, catching me staring.

"There's a game tonight?" I ask, trying to change the subject.

"Yeah," Derek answers now. "We don't usually go, though. Besides, you're going to the beach with us tonight, right?" His voice holds a note of unmistakable accusation.

I recognize the tone instantly. It's the tone of someone who has been let down, a lot. It's one I hear in my own voice sometimes. "I wouldn't miss it," I answer back, smiling.

Truthfully, I wasn't sure I'd have agreed to go if I'd known Oliver was playing that night. As silly as it sounds, I kinda like Oliver, and the idea that maybe he likes me too, well, all the better.

I feel myself blush, trying to decide whether to confide in my new—and only—girlfriend about hanging out with Oliver on Monday night. Twisting my hair around my index finger, I see something that makes the decision for me. As I watch from my driver's seat, a gorgeous blonde slips out of the passenger side of his truck. He closes the door for her, hefting her backpack onto his empty shoulder. They walk together toward the building, laughing and smiling.

A knife twists in my gut. Of course he has a girlfriend. What was I thinking? He isn't interested in me; he was just being nice, or being a total dog. I'm not sure which. My surprise quickly turns to indignation.

The first bell rings, and we gather our things and head inside. Reid catches up with me outside homeroom.

"So, how was your night?" he asks, handing me a plain white bag I know contains my daily glazed.

Reid looked much more relaxed than usual today. He often carries this almost-unnoticeable anxiety that makes his shoulders slump and his chin tilt downward. But not today.

"Uneventful," I reply. "Finished unpacking. Finally. You?"

"Oh, you know. A little of this, a little of that. You excited about tonight?" he ask.

Luckily, I'm busy digging my notebook out of my backpack when he asks, so he doesn't see the flash of annoyance cross my face. I'd have liked nothing better than to show up at the game tonight and call Oliver out in front of a crowd. It's an errant thought though; I know I'd never really do that, but it's a nice fantasy. I sigh, reminding myself it's not Reid I'm upset with, and I'd feel bad if he took it that way.

"Can't wait," I say, mustering my enthusiasm.

Kayla waves, and the boys exchange a head nod as we go our separate ways.

I don't talk to anyone else all morning, quickly darting past Oliver where he stands outside my first-period classroom. I don't know if he'd been waiting for me or not, and I don't look back. Lunch comes quickly and I take refuge in my small band of friends. Derek is leaning over his geometry notebook as Reid shows him how to solve whatever equation he's working on. Most of Reid's classes are Advanced Placement, including the chemistry class we share. As the resident brain of the group, he gets stuck tutoring the others a good deal, or so it seems. But he's always cool about it, always willing to lend a hand. No wonder Cassy has a thing for him. Reid might actually be the last genuinely good guy in the universe.

I grab my tray and scoot into my seat beside him. Unfortunately, today's cuisine—a scoop of something that could either be spaghetti or meatloaf—lacks the flavor of Monday's pizza. The word "surprise" in the name makes me regret not bringing something from home. I poke at it experimentally with my spork, looking for signs of life.

Kayla munches loudly on a chef's salad, which I eye enviously. "Where'd you get that?" I ask.

She points. "À la carte line. Over there."

I file that away for future use and take a bite of apple, the only semi-edible thing on my plate, while my lime-green Jell-O sloshes dejectedly. Derek is staring at me with an odd expression on his face. I hold out the apple. "You wanna bite?"

The side of his mouth twitches up like he might smile. "Apples are Satan's carbs."

I almost choke on my bite as I try not to laugh and fail. Reid sits up and pats my back gently. "Hey, you okay?" he asks. "I don't want to have to Heimlich you, but I will."

This just makes me laugh harder and in my peripheral vision, I see Oliver watching us. I lean forward, letting my hair fall loosely over the side of my face. "I'll live. I think."

He begins to fan me with his spiral notebook. "He's been staring at you all day," Reid says, following my gaze toward Oliver and back. "Did something happen?"

I sit up, fiddling with the stem of my apple. "Sort of. He... he kind of showed up at my house Monday night."

Reid stiffens. "Did he try anything?"

I wave my hand. "No, nothing like that. He just, I don't know. It was weird, he was being all nice, and then he was gone all week. I dunno. It's just weird."

I'm not going to tell them I fell for his charms. I'm not going to tell them that seeing him with another girl today hit me like a kick in the lady balls. And I'm certainly not going to tell them how stupid I feel about the whole thing now.

"Whatcha working on?" I ask, finally composing myself.

"Derek is pulling a C in biology. He needs at least a B," he says, slapping the book closed and stuffing it hurriedly into his backpack. "I took it last year so I'm helping him out."

"I've been meaning to ask you if you wanna be lab partners in chemistry," I mutter around another bite of apple.

"Yeah, because you two definitely have chemistry," Kara says with a wide, cheesy grin.

Derek elbows her in the ribs even as Reid groans and I roll my eyes.

"That was a bad joke," Reid says.

I nod. "Seriously bad. Not even a little punny."

She shrugs. "I do my best."

Beside her, Cassy pushes a scoop of mystery meat around her plate, not looking up. Bianca leans over, whispering something in her ear that makes her smile.

"You guys want a ride home after school? So I know where to pick everybody up tonight?" I ask, stealing a wedge of tomato from Kayla's salad and making her smile.

"Sure."

"Yeah."

"I walked today anyhow." Reid smiles. "Decided it would be faster."

We all laugh, because it's probably true.

"We'll meet at your car after school," Kayla says, stuffing the last bite of food into her mouth as the bell rings.

She and Derek walk hand in hand out of the cafeteria. I hang back, collecting my things with deliberate slowness. I've been trying, and failing, to not look at Oliver's table the whole half-hour. I'm trying to give him a window to apologize or explain himself or something. Unfortunately, Reid lags behind as well, determined to wait for me. After dumping the slimy contents unceremoniously in the tall, black trash can, I toss my empty tray in the return bin and head for the door.

We've made it all the way to the classroom door before I feel a hand on my shoulder.

"Where's the fire?" Oliver smiles, turning me toward him.

"Get lost," Reid says, knocking Oliver's hand off me.

Oliver's smile falters. "Excuse me, I'd like to have a word with Farris. I think whether or not I get lost is really up to her."

They both look at me expectantly. "You have two minutes," I tell Oliver. "Reid, I'll meet you in class."

"Yeah, she'll meet you in class," Oliver echoes, waving Reid off rudely, which only makes me angrier.

Reid looks annoyed, but he ducks into class, mumbling something rude and possibly four-lettered under his breath as he goes.

I shrug, trying to keep my face unreadable as I turn back to Oliver. "If you're trying to tick me off, being an asshole to my friends is a great place to start."

He holds up his hands. "Whoa. Sorry. But he kind of started it. I just wanted to say hello. I was out sick for a few days and I missed you."

I feel my eyes narrow. Oliver hasn't actually done anything wrong, not technically. It isn't like he made a pass at me or anything. Still, if I were his girlfriend, his getting friendly with another girl would be grounds for a serious nard kicking. I stare at him, trying to read his eyes. Is he one of those guys who flirts with everyone? Or is this just how he does nice?

"Hello, Earth to Farris. Do I have something on my face?" He chuckles uncomfortably.

I'm still staring intently at him, as if he were a bug under a microscope or a line of code. Those things I understand. Those things make sense to me. The boy in front of me does not. "I'm just trying to figure you out."

He breaks into a satisfied grin. "I'm not that complicated. But chicks dig the mysterious thing, so..."

I don't smile. I'm still waiting. Not sure for what, exactly.

"What do you want?" I ask finally. There are a hundred things running through my head to say, but to be honest, they all sound a little frazzled, so I just blink impatiently.

"Well, there's a game tonight, and I was wondering if you were going."

"Are you going?" I ask.

"Well, yeah, I'm kinda playing in it."

I blush. What, is my brain on *pause*? *He's not* that *cute*, I think grumpily. Only, he kind of is. Disarming. That's the word of the day. He's disarming.

"Oh yeah. Right," I mutter.

"So?" He waits.

"Uh, no. I have plans tonight actually," I say flippantly.

"With Reid?" he asks, annoyance finally creeping into his voice.

My hands tense on my chemistry book. That's what I need. Anger. If I can funnel that, I can use it to clear the cobwebs out of my brain. "That's not really any of your business, but yes. He and my other friends invited me to go to the Circle tonight. Why do you care?"

For a split second, Oliver looks like I slapped him. Maybe he just isn't used to losing.

Taking a step back, he visibly composes himself. "I thought we were having fun getting to know each other. Why the cold shoulder all of a sudden?" he asks, confused.

"We were, but maybe you should have mentioned in all that getting to know each other that you had a girlfriend," I snap, clutching my book to my chest.

For a minute, he looks even more confused, and then he laughs. "I don't have a girlfriend. Who told you that? Reid?"

My stomach churns. Have I really been a jerk all day for no reason? God, that is so like me.

"Um, I saw you with a girl this morning, at your truck," I fumble weakly.

"A pretty blonde?" he asks, shaking his head.

I nod, too mortified to speak.

"My sister, Georgia."

"Oh."

Blood rushes to my face, making the tips of my ears burn. *It's official. I'm the jerk.*

"So, now that we've established I am not involved in any form of committed relationship, why don't you come to the game?" He smiles, a single dimple blooming, and just like that, I'm forgiven.

I shift back and forth on my feet. "Like I said, I have plans."

"Break them," he says seriously.

I raise one eyebrow. "Why should I?"

He takes a deep breath, raking one hand through his hair before finally answering. "Reid... isn't the guy he seems to be. Seriously. I've known him a long time and—"

I stop him right there. "Just so you know, I've heard the same about you, from several people. Whatever this old drama is between you guys, I'm out of it. So I'll judge for myself who to spend time with."

He looks at me for a minute, a dozen different emotions swirling in his expression. Finally, he nods. "Fine. But why don't you come hang out with me Saturday? Some friends and I are having a thing."

"A thing? Like a party thing?"

He shrugs, "Sort of."

I bite my lip. It sounds like fun, but not only am I pretty busy all day Saturday, but the idea of going to a party... I mentally flip through my excuse list.

"You do owe me one now. For jumping to conclusions and blowing me off this morning after first period," he persuades, smiling. "In the spirit of judging for yourself and all."

"It's just, I just have lots of stuff to do on Saturday," I say apologetically. "And I'm not great with things. Gatherings. Parties. I kind of suck actually."

"I doubt that. But what do you have to do Saturday?" he asks, gently touching my elbow.

The feel of it makes my stomach flip again, but this time for a different reason. "Boring stuff. Laundry, new tags for my car, stuff like that."

"Ok, so I'll come over in the morning, help you run your errands, and then we'll hang out." It isn't a question, just a statement of fact.

"Do I get a choice?" I ask.

He shakes his head. "Not really. I mean, you can say no, but I think if you weren't at least as curious about me as I am about you, you wouldn't have been so upset when you thought I had a girlfriend."

His words make me blush so hard I think my hair might actually burst into flames. I say nothing. What can I say to that? He's totally right. And it irritates the shit out of me.

He leads me into class and deposits me next to Reid with a smirk. Reid ignores him, pulling open his laptop. Once again, five minutes with Oliver has left me completely shaken and half incoherent.

"You okay?" Reid mutters.

I nod, rubbing my eyes. "He's persistent, I'll give him that."

"That's one word for it."

THE AFTERNOON DRAGS THE WAY ONLY FRIDAY afternoons can, before the last bell finally sounds our freedom. Derek, Kayla, Bianca, and Reid are waiting for me beside my car by the time I make it outside.

"Cassy can't make it. She has Student Council tonight," Kala explains, loading everyone into the car.

As it turned out, Derek lives pretty close to me, just a few blocks over. If we were six-year-olds, we would have been comfortably in walkie-talkie range. I drop him off first, then Bianca, who is three doors down from Kayla. Reid lives in officer housing, which is just a mile or so from the school. His is a big, white house with an immaculate green lawn and blue-and-black patio furniture on the front deck.

"You wanna come in?" he asks when we arrive. "See what you can look forward to?"

"Sure," I say, pulling into the wide, oval driveway.

It is just as nice inside as I expected, and I feel a twinge of jealousy. The entryway is long with vaulted ceilings and hardwood floors—a stark contrast from my cold linoleum and faux tile. The only thing they have in common is the plain white paint scheme—well, that and the lack of pictures on the walls. There are a few framed paintings here and there, a motivational poster in the hall that reads "Discipline is the bridge between goals and accomplishments," but no family photos, no little plaster handprints, and no mementos of any kind. We walk down the hall, past a small table that holds one framed picture of his parents on their wedding day. They look young and happy, walking under a canopy of crossed swords in traditional Marine Corps style. He, strikingly similar in coloring to Reid, in his dress blues, a deceptive name for the black formal jacket, and she in a slender, simple white gown. My father has a similar photo on his nightstand, he and my mother on their wedding day. It's flanked by a photo of my first day of kindergarten when I was all pigtails and flower dresses. It makes me sad that there isn't a similar photo of him anywhere to be found.

No one is home as he gives me the tour. They have a media room that looks like a miniature movie theater, complete with two plush red armchairs and a square, tabletop popcorn maker. Reid's room is down the hall, and is more or less what I expected. The walls are covered in posters, a periodic table, original trilogy theater re-prints, one of a dinosaur with two grabby sticks that says unstoppable, and a poster of Albert Einstein sticking out his tongue. His desk is cluttered with notebooks and wadded-up papers, a sleek new laptop surrounded by empty Mountain Dew Code Red cans, and a glass filled with pens. Another table holds a Bunsen burner and some test tubes filled with colorful fluids. The shelf next to his bed is stuffed with trophies and medals. I pick one up and read the inscription.

"State karate finalist? I'm impressed. And a little afraid."

He grins, blushing fiercely, and rubs the back of his neck. "Yeah, it's not a big deal."

I sit down on the corner of his bed. It's big, probably queen sized, with thin, green camouflage blankets and pillows. He needs a new bed set as much as I do. "Nice place," I say as I bounce a bit.

He shrugs. "Its home."

For all its comforts, it doesn't feel very homey to me. It feels awkward. Uncomfortable. "I'd better get going. I need to clean up before we go out tonight."

Reid walks me to the door, gives me a short goodbye, and shuts the door as I walk to my car. The afternoon sun is strong and hot, and it's made my interior uncomfortably warm. Leaning across the seat, I roll down the passenger window before driving away. Tucked into the seat is one of Derek's collar studs. Must have fallen off at some point, I realize, rolling it between my fingers. Stuffing it in my pocket, I make mental note to take it over tonight.

I drop by Dad's new office on the way home, as requested. The shiny new hangar with the static jet fighter on display out front makes it difficult to miss. This base holds three types of aircraft and ten squadrons. The A-6 is the ugliest of the three. It's big, it's loud, and it looks like there's a weird horn protruding from the front of its grey hull. But its job is electronic countermeasures—a fancy term for radar jamming. The second aircraft on base is the Harrier, best known for being in an Arnold Schwarzenegger movie once. They are sleek and cool looking, and have the ability to hover in midair. They also fall out of the sky so often the locals call them Carolina lawn darts. Then there's the JSF. It is the best of both worlds. It's sleek, maneuverable, smart, and more than capable of making any foreign leader wet himself. It is also still relatively new and the only squadron on base that has any is now under my father's command.

After clearing security, I pass the on-call office, a tiny, closet-like office near the door that right now is empty. I frown. I'd hoped to get directions from the on-call duty officer, but apparently I'm on my own. The hallways aren't complicated but they all look the same, so finding one particular door could be a challenge.

Half an hour later, I finally locate the steel door marked CO for Commanding Officer. I open the heavy, grey door and find myself face to face with a man I have to assume is Reid's father. It's strange seeing him, after just being in his house, looking at his wedding photo, feels a bit stalker-ish. He's still incredibly handsome, with a square chin and broad shoulders. He has Reid's friendly green eyes. Or is that the other way around?

Maybe it's just the flight suit, but I have to clear my throat because my mouth's gone dry looking at him. It's kind of cliché to swoon over a man in uniform, but these things become cliché for a reason.

I must be staring at him like an idiot because he smiles and grabs me gently by my shoulders, moving me to the side so he can pass.

"Hey, kid, come on in," my dad yells from the other side of a frosted glass door emblazoned with his name and rank.

His office is nice, in a generic Marine Corps kind of way. A few flags, some uncomfortable-looking aluminum chairs, and a wide, cherry desk complete with computer, phone, and decorative, pen-sized flag set. He sits in his high-backed chair and motions for me to come in as I poke my head in the doorway.

He's on the phone, and I can hear tension in his voice. "Yes, sir. No, sir. No, I don't believe this is anything of importance. Yes, sir, they've been notified," he says, using his official tone.

I try to ignore the one-sided conversation, but

my natural curiosity gets the better of me and I catch myself trying to make out the barely audible buzzing of the voice on the other end of the phone. It's too low to pick out more than a few words. I catch *investigation*, *report*, and *email*, but nothing to connect them. I take a step forward to get closer to the sound, but Dad stops me with an upheld hand. He knows me so well.

He points at the maroon couch on the far wall, so I take a seat, pulling the strap of my messenger bag over my head, and wait till he hangs up.

"So, you want the official tour?" he ask, standing and offering me his hand.

"Actually, I already got it. I got a little lost on my way up here, and either I saw the whole squadron once, or I saw one hallway twelve times," I admit.

He sits back down. "Probably for the best. I'm swamped here. We were supposed to get a shipment of pre-seal today and ended up with three crates of pudding instead."

I feel my eyes widen. "Pudding? Was it an accident or are you guys planning some Animal House-style shenanigans up in the base pool?"

He rubs his face in his hands. "It's been like this since before I got here. They brought me in to fix this shit but now..." He cocks his head to the side, cracking his neck before rolling his head and repeating it on the other side. There's clearly more, but he's not sharing.

I decide to prod just a little. "And that's it? It's just ordering issues?"

He shakes his head. "I wish. The duty roster keeps glitching out and don't even get me started on the flight schedule. As of right now, I have ten planes in the hangar with nobody on them, and no flights going because the computer is showing them all as needing inspections."

I frown. "That sounds like a computer problem. You got someone looking at it?"

He nods again. "Yeah, we got a team coming in this weekend to do a system overhaul. Hopefully, they can take care of it."

I glance at his desktop. It's not surprising they are having issues; the thing is probably ten years old. It's thick, wide, loud, and the once-white shell has yellowed with age. "Maybe you just need to let these dinosaurs die and move into the twenty-first century," I say.

He frowns. "It's the twenty-second century."

I raise an eyebrow. "Exactly."

He grunts dismissively, and I know exactly what the sound means. It means there is no way he can find it in the budget to requisition new computers.

"You all right on your own tonight?" he asks. "I'm going to be pretty late."

I stand, slinging my bag across my torso. "No problem. I'll grab something to eat on the way to the Circle."

"What exactly is this *Circle*? It's not some trendy nightclub, is it?" he asks, unable to fully keep the worry from his voice.

I bite my lip, remembering that night not so long ago. *Pauline was a six-foot-two Amazon with long, dirty-blonde hair and serious daddy issues that had her chasing after any guy who looked twice at her. She was also my best friend. When she wanted to go to a party at Dayan Montgomery's house, I was all in. Just being invited as a freshman was a big deal, and he was a gorgeous lacrosse god besides. Somewhere along the way, she decided it'd be fun to roll some molly. I'd been drinking and when I found her a few hours later, she was passed out cold under the pool table, blood trickling out of her nose and mouth. Dayan and some of the others wanted to toss her in the car and let her sleep it off, but I knew something was wrong. I called an ambulance and the EMTs called the cops. Nineteen of us were busted for underage drinking that night, and Dayan was also caught holding some weed and molly. Turned out, Pauline had just hit the side of the table when she passed out, making her nose bleed. She was fine, pissed and stoned, but fine. They didn't put me in jail, I wasn't even officially charged, but they called Dad to come get me. While we were busy cleaning up my mess at the police station, Mom died in her sleep.*

I'm not sure even now if Dad has ever really forgiven me for that, but I sure as hell haven't forgiven myself.

"It's an amusement park at the beach from what I gather," I say, trying to keep my tone light. "But if you'd rather I find some trendy nightclub to patronize..."

He waves me off as his phone rings again. "Sure, whatever. Have fun."

Spinning on my heel, I stride out of the office, making it all the way back to my car before I feel the first tear fall.

FIVE

A FTER THE WORLD'S QUICKEST SHOWER, I CHANGE into my favorite patchwork blue jeans and a white tank top with an *I*, a heart, and a picture of Darth Vader on the front. What can I say? I'm a sucker for the redeemably evil.

Dad still hasn't made it home by the time I leave to pick everyone up. "Sweet Jane" is playing on the radio when I pull up to Derek's house, an oldie but a goodie. I crank the volume.

Waiting for me, Derek is wearing black pants and a blood-red shirt with frilly sleeves and red lace down the front. It strikes me as strange that he's was sitting outside in the dim glow of the porch light alone, but when he opens the car door to get in, I understand. Even over the stereo, I can hear the shouting coming from inside his house. A man's voice, then a woman's, then a man's again. At that volume, it will only be a matter of time before the Military Police show up. Derek's face is hard and stiff, shut down. He stares straight ahead, not speaking. He doesn't even take a breath until we're out of sight of his house.

"You okay?" I ask gently.

He nods. I hold out his tiny silver stud, and he takes it with long, slender fingers.

"It's my dad. He's kind of an asshole when he drinks." He smiles humorlessly. "And when he doesn't drink."

I say nothing, but crank the radio a little louder, as if I can somehow drown the voices I know he's hearing inside his own head.

It's a short drive from there to Kayla's. She's chattering away as soon as she gets into the car. Listening to her ramble about a new movie that just came out, I see why Derek likes her so much. She's human white noise, a constant voice to cut through the uncomfortable silence. I wonder if she realizes that she is exactly what he needs, the missing piece to his life puzzle. I also wonder if I'll ever find someone who could be that for me. Someone who knows what I need without being told.

Even with her loud, pink hot-pants and oversized, zebra-print top, she is pretty. Her now-wavy hair is pulled back into a ponytail, showing off her long, silver earrings. Upon closer inspection, they turn out to be miniature razor blades dangling from her lobes.

"Bianca can't come. Her family is making her go to some party for her grandmother or something.

So it's just us," Kayla says cheerfully, zooming right back into describing the movie in detail for Derek.

Reid is also waiting outside for us when we pull up. He has on a pair of chinos and a white collared shirt with the top buttons open. A pair of black Chuck Taylor sneakers completes the look. He looks hot, standing there with his hands in his pockets. *Clark Kent hot*, I think with a smirk. When I pull up, he runs a hand through his dark brown hair and waves, making my heart stutter just a little.

Derek and Kayla happily squeeze into the backseat, leaving Reid and I inches apart, our arms barely touching across the middle console. Where his flesh grazes mine, goose bumps break out across my skin.

"Hey, you clean up nice," I say.

"You're not too shabby yourself," Reid jokes before leaning his head back to talk to the others. "You guys eat yet?"

"Nope," Derek answers.

"Me neither," Kayla chimes in.

"I had a snack, but I could eat," I say when he turns to me.

"Let's hit Bayside before we head for the beach," he suggests.

Kayla groans, rolling her eyes.

"What's Bayside?" I ask curiously.

"It's an institution," Reid answers, his expression serious.

"Yeah, if you're talking about the quality of the food." Kayla snorts.

Reid waves her off. "Pay no attention to her. The food's good, the atmosphere's great, and they have the best coffee in town."

Kayla groans again as we pull through the main gate, Reid directing me as we go.

REID WAS RIGHT ABOUT THE COFFEE, BUT KAYLA WAS right about the food, so it's a toss-up. There is definitely something to be said for the greasy-spoon restaurant with its bright yellow booths and greenish walls. The waitress, whose name tag actually reads "Flo," is sweet and keeps the coffee coming. I don't drink coffee often, but it is warm and good, and by the time we leave, I'm feeling a touch jittery.

The Circle is about a twenty-minute drive away, so it's dark by the time we arrive. I'm almost afraid we're lost when, over the horizon, a sparkling, twinkling, well-lit wonderland emerges. We park a few blocks down the boardwalk and hike back to the large roundabout that is known simply as the Circle. There's a Ferris wheel, some bumper boats, and even go-karts. It's like a circus that never leaves town. People laugh and music crackles through overhead speakers, not quite drowning out the sound of the waves crashing in the distance.

It's amazing.

"So what do you want to do first?" Reid asks, turning to me.

I stare in wonder at the rides and games, trying to decide. It's so crowded and so bright that I can't quite take it all in. "Let's ride the big wheel. I want to see this from up high," I suggest.

He breaks into a pleased grin and leads me to the line.

"Heights aren't really my thing," Kayla says apologetically before tugging Derek by the hand and vanishing into the crowd.

I wonder if she's truly afraid of heights, or whether it's just her not-so-subtle way of giving Reid and me some privacy. I cringe internally. Reid is handsome, sweet, and genuinely fun. So what is my problem? *Just go for it*, the *before* voice whispers in my head. I smile, forcing myself to relax.

"So, I have to ask, your name, Farris, is there a story behind that?" he asks.

I shake my head, tucking a strand of hair behind my ear. "No, it's not Ferris like Ferris wheel. It's from *Ferris Bueller's Day Off*. My mom had a thing for the movie."

Reid hands our tickets to the burly ride operator and helps me into a seat with his hand at the small of my back. As he closes the metal rail over our laps, I see a familiar face in the crowd. It was the small, blonde girl, Oliver's sister, sitting on a bench eating an ice cream cone. If I didn't know better, I'd have sworn she was looking right at me. I don't have time to stare at her for long because soon we are being lifted into the sky. I turn my eyes away for just a second, watching the reflection of the lights dancing on the crisp water rolling in and out on the sand beyond, and when I look back, she's disappeared into the sea of people beneath me. If she is here, does that mean Oliver is here somewhere, too? Is it possible the game is over already?

"Are you okay? You look distracted," Reid observes.

"I thought I saw Oliver's sister down there. I can't remember her name."

"It's Georgia. Like the state," he says with a slight frown.

"That's right. Sorry, it was bugging me. I'm kinda bad with names."

He's still frowning. *This is gonna kill me*, I decide, taking a deep breath.

SIX

"OKAY, WHAT'S THE DEAL WITH YOU TWO?" I demand, folding my arms over my chest. "I was gonna stay out of it, but it's obviously the huge woolly mammoth in the room. So, I think I deserve to know."

"Who? Me and Georgia?" he asks, looking stunned.

"No, you and Oliver. What's with all the animosity? You two get within three feet of each other and the tension gets thick enough to drown in."

Reid leans forward, rocking the small cart. We are almost at the top of the wheel, the salty breeze from the nearby beach dancing in my hair. I wish I'd put it in a ponytail instead of letting it hang free, but the wind feels good, even as it tumbles my hair into gentle knots.

Finally, Reid turns, looking straight into my eyes as he speaks. "I wasn't going to say anything because I know you like him, and I didn't want to come off as a jerk or anything. If you really want to know, I'll tell you, but it has to stay between us."

His tone is clipped, but his expression is still hesitant, as if he wants to tell me, but also doesn't want to. Must be serious, I realize, giving Reid a brisk nod.

He relaxes back into the seat, turning his eyes to the cloudy sky above us and begins. "We used to be best friends when we were little. Oliver's dad is a Navy doc stationed here, so they don't move around like the rest of us. We used to make mud pies in his backyard." He smiles sadly at the memory. "I moved away when I was six, and then after my parents' tour in California was over, we got stationed back here again."

With a deep sigh, he leans forward, clasping his hands over the railing. "I was fourteen by then, and I thought we'd be friends again, just like we were before. It was freshman year and he was the new superjock on the football team. At first, he acted like he didn't even know me. He was always in some kind of trouble, fighting mostly. He used to pick on me mercilessly for anything he could think of. One day, I caught up with him in the locker room after gym class. He was taking pills out of a prescription bottle with the label torn off. When he saw me, he shoved them into his locker and slammed it shut. When I asked what he was doing, he freaked out. Said it was none of my business and that if I said anything about it, he'd make my life a living hell."

Wow. "Did you ever find out what the pills were?"

He shakes his head. "I figured he was taking something illegal. Steroids or something. Who knows? The crazy thing was, I didn't even care. I just wanted my friend back." He pauses, his eyes sweeping the crowd below. "I went to his house that night, to... I dunno. Make up or apologize. Something. Georgia was there. She's a year older than us, you know, and she'd always been nice to me. Anyway, I told her about the pills and she called me a liar, slapped me in the face and told me to get out before she called the cops. Oliver showed up right about then, and he wailed on me for a while before literally kicking me out the front door. And that was that."

I try to process his story. It seems so different from the person I know now, but then, how well do I really know Oliver at all? "Wow." I'm not sure there's anything more I can say.

He shrugs. "Thing is, I swore I'd never say anything. He may be a total dick now, but he wasn't always."

I nod, an unspoken vow of silence. Steroids? Pain killers? Something else? Was he still using or had he gotten clean? The ride is going full swing now, which is still painfully slow. My mind races; I want my body to be moving fast, too. Maybe it will help me process what he's just told me. I try to shrug it off, for now. No reason to spoil a perfectly good evening by stressing about things I can't deal with right now anyway.

I want to thank Reid for trusting me, for telling me the truth, but I don't. I look at him, my expression soft but serious. "Go-karts next?" I ask.

He laughs, the tension falling off him like shedding water. "Whatever you want, Farris."

We hook back up with Derek and Kayla and ride the go-karts, get some smoothies and walk on the beach, carefully avoiding the nearly invisible fiddler crabs scurrying underfoot in the intermittent moonlight. Reid and I talk about books, bands, and cars. I check my phone only once, for the time, and see a missed call from an unknown number. Clicking it off, I slide it back into my pocket.

The noise from the Circle fades into the distance as we amble along the water's edge. The beach is practically empty as we make our way past the shops and bustle of the boardwalk. The full moon sparkles where it reflects atop the quivering water for a few moments before once more being swallowed by the dark sky. Realizing we've lost sight of Derek and Kayla, we sit down, taking off our shoes and letting the cold, foamy surf roll up onto our feet.

"Did you have a good night?" he asks, lifting his face skyward.

I nod. "I really did. Thanks. And thank you for being honest with me before."

He tilts his head. "No one is perfect, you know? We all have our issues. But it really sucks to lose a friend." He takes a breath, holding it before blowing it out hard. "And when a friend turns on you, it's the worst thing ever. Because then it's war, and they know just where to hit you. They know where all your weak spots are."

Boy, don't I know it.

"Ferris wheel. That's what they called me. You know, like, everyone gets a ride." I take a deep breath of my own, doodling in the sand with my finger so I don't have to meet his gaze when he looks back to me. "It wasn't true, of course, just another way to make me suffer. There was this party freshman year, it turned into an ugly night, and I had to make a judgment call. Sometimes I wonder if I did the right thing," I admit. "I've never told anyone about this—well, except my therapist. But sometimes I wonder, if I could do it again, would I make the same choice? And if I say no, what kind of person does that make me?"

I feel his hand on mine, stilling it from completing the next circle in the sand. Glancing up, I meet his eyes. "You can't second-guess yourself. We all have to make decisions, and sometimes they suck and we screw things up six ways to Sunday. But those choices define us, show us who we are. All we can do is our best."

In that heartbeat, I feel a spark, a connection

I can't quite explain. Like he understands me. Not just the face I show to everyone else, but the stuff underneath, all the screwed-up stuff, the damaged-beyond-repair stuff, the ugly stuff I can't bring myself to admit. It's like he sees it, and there's no judgment.

The relief floods me like a tidal wave. I didn't realize how badly I needed someone to understand, someone to hold my hand and tell me it was ok. I was ok. Staring into his gentle, blue eyes, I imagine, just for a moment, leaning forward and placing a kiss on his velvety lips. I might not have been able to control the urge if not for Kayla and Derek appearing behind us. Hearing them, he turns away, and the spell is broken. I blink, as if coming out of a trace. He squeezes my hand once before standing and dusting the sand off his butt. I follow suit.

"You guys ready to go?" Derek asks. "Kayla has a midnight curfew."

By the time we reach the car, I'm so tired, and I decide to let Reid drive home. Maybe it was the sleepless nights I've been having all week, or the sheer emotional exhaustion at finally sharing my secret with someone, but either way, I am spent. Handing over my keys to Reid earns me a look of surprise from Kayla.

"You okay?" she asks, thrusting a hand to my forehead.

I nod blearily. "Just tired."

We drop Derek and Kayla off at Kayla's house. Apparently, Derek slept over often, less a romantic situation than an emotional one, if I had to guess. Reid offers to drive me home and walk back to his house, but I refuse. The last thing I want is for him to have to walk home in the dark, autumn chill.

We pull into his driveway just before midnight, which meant I'd be a solid five minutes late on my own curfew.

"Well, thanks. I had a really good time tonight," I say, climbing back into the driver's seat.

"Me, too. You wanna hang out tomorrow?" he asks. "Cassy is coming over to watch movies around three."

Part of me really wants to say yes. Being with him and the others tonight, I'd felt more normal than I have in a really long time. Still, I know Cassy is looking for a little one-on-one time so I bite my lip. "I can't. Maybe another time?"

"Sure. See you later." His head droops just a little. "And, whatever you have going on with Oliver, just... just be careful. Maybe he's changed, maybe he's just an asshole to me, but if he ever did anything to hurt you..." He doesn't finish the thought.

I press my lips into a flat line and tilt my head in a silent thank you.

Patting the hood of the car once, he turns on his heel and walks up his porch steps, flicking the light off behind him as he goes inside.

In the five minutes it takes me to get home, my brain hits hyperdrive. I believe Reid is telling me the truth about Oliver, about what he saw, but at the same time, I'd been wrong jumping to conclusions before, and I don't want to do it again. Maybe I can just talk to him about it, find some clever way of bringing it up. Or maybe I'll just be cautious, keep my eyes open and my guard up. It's just hard since anytime I get around him, my IQ drops twenty points.

I sigh, clutching the wheel even after I've parked and removed the key from the ignition, and stare into the dark front window of my house. Only a faint flicker of white light tells me Dad is home and awake, no doubt waiting for me.

So how sick is it that despite all that, despite the fact I'd very nearly thrown myself at Reid not an hour ago, despite my reservations about Oliver's character, that I'm still looking forward to spending the day with him tomorrow? What does that say about me?

SEVEN

THAT NIGHT I DREAMED.

Reid and I are on the Ferris wheel, only the park is empty, eerily still against the veil of darkness. There's a sound, a low, rhythmic heartbeat that seems to make the air around us contract with each beat. We aren't moving, just sitting at the very top, the metal rail across my lap holding me in place. Reid has his fingers in my hair, his body pressing firmly against mine as our mouths connect. Then there's a feeling, an odd tugging inside my mind as if someone is watching me, the tiny hairs on the back of my neck standing up. I pull back and Reid trails kisses down my neck, ignoring me. I search for a face in the darkness. Praying it isn't Oliver, I squint, scanning the tangle of sidewalks below us. *Please, not Oliver*, I think. The idea of him seeing me kissing Reid is making me frantic, though I'm not completely sure why.

Finally, my eyes lock onto the single upturned face. It's Georgia, Oliver's sister.

She's standing beneath us, pointing at me and shouting, but even though there is no other sound, I can't hear her. Leaning further away from Reid, I strain to hear, to try to make out the curve of her mouth, hoping to guess at her words, but it's no use. I turn back to Reid, looking for help, but he's gone. Now alone in the darkness, I sit, paralyzed with fear as the tiny cart rocks precariously, the unseen press of the heartbeat growing until I can feel it in my bones.

Georgia is gone now, too, I realize dreamily. Carefully sliding out from under the bar, I climb down the side of the ride, jungle-gym style. It feels like I'm descending forever. My arms ache, sweat rolling down my face and stinging my eyes. *How tall is this damn thing?* Looking down, I see a new face staring up at me. My mother, her long hair billowing around her face, is looking up at me, disappointment in her eyes. I try to cry out to her. *Help me!* I shout inside my head, no voice passing my lips. Georgia walks over and my mother puts a hand on her shoulder as she points up at me and says something I can't hear.

Tears burn my eyes. I fumble through the bars, nearly losing my grip. Near the bottom of what was now a dangerously high ladder, my foot slips. I start to fall when a hand shoots down from above me and latches onto my arm. When I looked up, it's Oliver's smiling face above me. He's saying something that sounds like "I've got you." Suddenly, Reid is beside him, his hand clamping onto my other arm. A crack of lighting streaks across the sky, blinding me for a heartbeat before the rolling boom of thunder echoes in my ears. Rain begins to pour, cold and stinging my bare flesh. The boys fight to hold me, tugging me back and forth between them. I try to scream, but it's swallowed by another roll of thunder. My arms wet, the rain rolls off me, and I slip from both their grips. The last thing I remember is falling into an abyss of dark, churning water.

THE NEXT MORNING, I WAKE UP TO MY FATHER'S voice. "Get up, sleepyhead, breakfast!"

Groaning, I kick my covers off, slip into my fluffy, purple robe, and shuffle to the kitchen, fully prepared to complain about being summoned so early on a Saturday. But as I round the corner, I freeze, taking a good ten seconds to process what I see. My father is fully dressed in his uniform, with a camouflaged apron that reads *Grillmaster* in white letters tied over it. He's serving a stack of fresh pancakes to someone seated at our table. Though part of me recognized him even from the back of his head, it's not until he turns and catches sight of me that the real horror sinks in.

Oliver.

With a very girlie yelp, I spin and press my back

against the hallway wall. Laughter rolls out from the other room from both of them. Part of me wants to stride back in, chin up, and pretend I don't care that he just witnessed my bed-head and ratty grey pajama pants. The other part of me really wants to go brush my teeth and put on a bra.

It wins out.

"Just a minute!" I yell, making a beeline for the bathroom and slamming the door closed behind me.

What was Oliver doing here so early, anyway? I wonder, mentally cursing him as I rinse out the last bits of minty toothpaste.

Pulling my phone from my robe pocket, I see it's after nine. I overslept, but it feels like I was awake all night, kicking and screaming. My muscles ache and my throat is sore. Furiously, I tug on a pair of denim shorts and a black tank top, run a brush through my knotted hair, and pull it into a high ponytail. I slip into a pair of white low-top Chucks and tuck my wallet into my back pocket. Pausing at my door, I open it just a crack, straining to hear if they are talking. There are voices coming from the kitchen, but they are too muffled to make out.

Oh, God. What is my father saying to him?

I was going to put on a little makeup, but my priorities have quickly shifted from getting myself put together to not letting them be alone any longer. I'm practically sprinting back down the hall when Oliver steps out of the kitchen, too late for me to

.

slow down. I hit him at full speed, but he manages to keep his feet, laughing.

"Ouch! We could use a hitter like you on the line. You ever think of playing football?" he asks, holding me by my arms as he peels me off his chest.

"I don't do well with helmet hair," I quip, recovering myself quickly. I look around him to my dad, who chuckles. "What are you boys talking about?" I say, looking back at Oliver suspiciously.

His eyes widen, looking at me seriously. "Your dowry. I gotta say, three cows and a goat? I could do better."

He releases my arms and I walk around him, letting the smell of pancakes and bacon guide me.

"You hungry, kid?" Dad asks.

"Nah. I had a Tic-Tac earlier. I'm fine."

Dad holds a plate of pancakes out to me, and I snatch them from his hand. The smell of butter and maple hangs in the air, making my stomach gurgle with anticipation. I smile at Oliver and take a chair at the table. He sits down beside me, nursing a glass of orange juice.

"The boy was just telling me you're going to a party today," Dad says, his tone bemused.

I flinch, remembering I hadn't exactly asked permission. "Um, yeah. That's the plan. After I do my chores and stuff," I add, hoping to sound more responsible than I feel.

He looks over his cup of coffee to Oliver, who is

sitting quietly. "And you're going to help her do her chores, I guess?"

Oliver nods once. "Yes, sir. I'm a firm believer that no one should ever have to do laundry alone."

Dad turns his back to us, pouring the last of the batter onto the griddle. Oliver winks at me behind his back.

"Besides," Oliver continues. "It's not really a party. Just a few of my friends from the team getting together."

That makes me shift in my seat. The smaller the group, the more I would have to interact. I wasn't exactly a people person, and none of the kids from his table had so much as introduced themselves to me in school yet—meaning things could go from zero to awkward real fast.

"Just as well, I have to go into the office today anyway," Dad mutters.

Shoving the last bite of pancake into my mouth I stride over, leaning in as I slip my plate in the sink. "Everything ok?" I ask.

He shrugs. "The tech support team is coming back today. They are saying it's just a system glitch. Hope to have everything ironed out by Monday. But it means wiping several of the main computers. And of course, I have to be there to supervise."

I nod. "Ok. And if you need any help..." I trail off. He knows I'm probably better than anyone the DOJ is bringing in, but neither of us says it.

"Go, have a good day." He jerks his head toward Oliver, his back to us, still sitting at the table.

After breakfast we load three bags of laundry into the back of Oliver's truck. I protest, but he points out that if I put them in my car, there'd be no room for him to sit, so I relent. His truck is surprisingly spacious and smells vaguely of peanuts and leather. We drive to the coin laundry by the Exchange. His radio blares They Might Be Giants the whole way— one of my favorite bands ever—and we both sing at the top of our lungs.

Standing on the back tire in the parking lot outside the launderette, I heft the bags out of the truck bed and toss them to Oliver. He stacks them in a rolling cart, which he then rides inside like a cowboy. The place is fairly crowded with Marines doing laundry on their off days—yes, this is the glamorous life of our country's finest. Luckily, I spot two washers side by side, and we swoop in. There's no way I'm going to let Oliver help with this part so I send him next door to the Exchange for laundry soap. He returns just as I finish separating the clothes into the two machines. We pour in the soap, feed the machines a truly obscene amount of quarters, and close the lids. He hops up on one, leaning forward onto his arms.

"So, now what?" he asks.

"Now we wait, I guess," I say, frowning. The only table is full and the TV is set to the news station. I consider offering to go get a cup of coffee or something, but Oliver seems so full of energy I'm afraid his heart might explode from the added caffeine.

"I've got a better idea, come on." He slides off the washer and grabs me by the hand.

"Are you sure my stuff's safe if we leave it?" I ask as we climb into his truck.

"Oh, I think a room full of Marines can handle any dirty-sock ninjas that might sneak in and try to steal your unmentionables," he jokes.

"Dirty-sock ninjas?" I ask, narrowing my eyes at him.

He shrugs. "It pays to specialize. Even for ninjas."

We drive off base to the pool hall just outside the main gate. The neon sign flashes "BJ's Billiards." It looks small from the outside, but once you get in the door, it really opens up. There are probably twenty tables, a foosball room, and a long, wooden bar. The odor of stale beer and cigarettes hangs in the air, that, combined with the musty scent of old felt and chalk, makes my nose tingle like I need to sneeze, but can't.

Oliver waves to the bartender, an older man with grey hair and a long, thin face, and picks up a tray of balls before crossing the room, taking a pool cue down from the wall, and handing it to me.

"You play?" he asks.

"A little," I lie.

My dad's table is still in storage—curse you, enlisted housing—but I learned to play when I was little. I am pretty good, too, if I do say so myself.

We take up residence at an empty table in the corner, far from the handful of other patrons hanging out closer to the front of the room. I run my hand over the table, feeling the texture of the cherry wood, the worn brass pockets and leather catches. The felt is still bright green, probably newly refinished as the leather inside the pockets is well worn.

Oliver puts the balls on the table and sets the rack.

"So what are we playing for?" I ask, chalking my stick.

"Tell you what, new girl, if you sink one, you get to ask me a question. Any question. If I sink one, I get to ask. Deal?"

I smirk, shaking his outstretched hand. "Deal."

Oliver sets the balls in careful order and removes the plastic triangle. I position the cue ball, leaning over and strike.

I sink one on the break. "Okay," I ask, "if you could live anywhere, where would you live?"

Oliver leans on his pool cue, his mouth twitching. "I don't know. There are so many places I want to see... Scotland, maybe."

"You'd look good in a kilt," I say.

He nods. "I know, I've been gifted with god-like

calves."

I shoot again and the ball rattles in the pocket, not falling in. He takes his turn, sinking one.

"Ok," he begins, tapping his chin as if trying to come up with a question. "Who was your first kiss?"

I feel myself tense. Jack. Or Jack Ass, as I refer to him now. He'd been my boyfriend freshman year. That was before. Before I'd become public enemy number one. Before he'd started all kinds of terrible rumors about me. Before I taught myself not to care.

When I open my mouth, I'm honestly not sure what I'm going to say. Am I going to lie? Telling him all about my sordid past doesn't feel the same as telling Reid. How can he ever understand what I went through? He's obviously been attractive and popular his whole life. I shift from foot to foot.

"I don't remember." The lie comes out jerky and obvious.

He looks at me, blinking once, but doesn't press further.

The game continues and after I've beaten him twice, I know pretty much everything there is to know about the boy. The name of his first pet, his biggest regret, and a dozen other things only a good identity thief would care about. I know everything except the one thing burning in the back of my brain, the question aching to be asked. Is what Reid said true? I can't force myself to bring it from my mouth.

"Where'd you learn to play?" he asks after paying our tab.

"Dad taught me. He was sort of a hustler back in the day from what I understand." I snicker, the idea of my straitlaced father doing something as undignified as hustling pool was almost too much.

"You know, I think you actually just told me something about yourself without my having to pry it out of you."

So I had.

"Don't get used to it," I say jokingly, pulling the door open for him.

"Wouldn't dream of it."

We get back to the laundry mat just in time to take advantage of some empty dryers. After loading the soggy clothes, Oliver picks me up, tosses me gently into the rolling basket, and wheels me around the room. I laugh so hard my eyes water with delight. When I climb out, I notice the stern look from the squat woman behind the counter. My foot catches in the cart and I nearly fall on my butt, making Oliver roar with laughter as he comes to my rescue. He catches me in his arms, holding me there just a little longer than is strictly necessary, his eyes locked onto mine, sending my heart into frantic spasms. For a second, I think he might kiss me, making my heart beat even faster. I watch as the intent flickers across his face, and then passes. He smiles awkwardly, the dimple appearing in the side of his face, and gently pushes me away. The disappointment is sharp and surprising as he releases me.

We spend the next hour playing on our phones in weird silence. Then, I get a text.

Is everything okay?

I glance up and see Oliver staring at me over the top of his phone, which he's holding near his nose.

I'm good, I text back.

He nods.

If you had a genie, and could wish for any three things, what would you wish for?

I stare at his text, chewing on my bottom lip as I answer.

High-speed Wi-Fi, a pet giraffe-pug hybrid, and...

I pause, my fingers hesitating over the keypad.

My mom back.

I quickly delete the last words and replace them with: *a working TARDIS*.

He smirks, and three minutes later sends me a really inappropriate giraffe GIF and I laugh so hard I snort.

When the laundry is finished, I stuff it into the bags and we haul them back to my house. There's a note from Dad stuck to the fridge.

Kid,

I took care of the new tags for your car. Go have fun today. Remember what I said about the boy.

Love, Dad

I crumple up the note before Oliver can read it

and ask embarrassing questions.

"What's next on the agenda?" he asks, swiping a bottle of water from my fridge as I toss the bags into the living room. I'll fold the clothes later.

"It looks like that's it. My dad took care of the other stuff. I'm all yours." As soon as the words fall out of my mouth, I regret them. Mostly because they are ridiculously true.

His eyes sparkle with delight. "Well then, let's head to the park."

Oliver holds his hand out to me and smiles that devastating smile. How bad can a little party be? I can do this, I decide, steeling myself. *Maybe it's a bad idea*, some small part of my brain whispers. Looking into his face, I decide I don't really care.

THE DAY IS WARM BUT OVERCAST, A SOFT HAZE hanging across the sky, obscuring the sun so only a muffled glow escapes. "You gonna tell me where we're going?"

He keeps his eyes glued to the road, swinging the truck onto a narrow, semi-wooded street. "We're going to Centennial Park," he says, offering nothing more than that. My stomach growls; it's too late for lunch but too soon for dinner, making me wish I stuffed a granola bar in my bag before leaving the house.

Finally, the pine trees thin and a group of picnic

benches sit under a wooden canopy. Several cars are parked in the nearby gravel lot as we pull in beside them. There's a small playground to the north, looking derelict and abandoned. A single swing blows in the soft breeze.

As soon as I open my door, the scent of charcoal and gas wafts in my direction. Someone is grilling, and the not-unpleasant smell makes my stomach clench hungrily. Someone has music playing, old-school classic rock beating though a single black speaker, loud enough to hear, but not so loud as to be overwhelming. Rounding the truck quickly, Oliver closes my door and takes hold of my hand, leading me toward the group.

The pavilion is crammed, but it isn't the number of people that makes it feel crowded as much as the average size of the occupants. It looks like half the football team has shown up, and the smallest of them is still a comfortable five foot eleven, probably two hundred plus pounds of lean muscle. There are girls too, some faces I recognize from Oliver's lunch table at school, a few others I've seen in class. Bianca is there too, her nose stuck in a sleek, white laptop. I wave, but she doesn't look up to see.

"We won last night," Oliver explains, leaning in close and whispering in my ear. "This is sort of a tradition. Post-victory barbeque."

I blink at him. I've been to lots of parties in my time, everything from pool parties to cheesy college raves. Never something quite as mellow as this. There's not even a keg, I realize, looking around. I feel the tension slip from my shoulders, an invisible ball of dread I've been carrying falling away at the scene. Oliver must sense my relief because he grins, squeezing my hand.

When we arrive, there is the typical amount of macho fist bumps and posturing. I recognize Georgia, sitting on the lap of the tallest guy. He's lanky with sandy-blond hair and a long, narrow chin. She nods to me, a friendly smile spreading across her face. The picnic tables are gray and splintered with age. In the center of the table where they sit is a small cardboard box filled with bags of buns, condiments, and paper plates. To my surprise, Oliver's arm snakes around my shoulder as he introduces me to the crowd.

"Everybody, this is Farris. Farris, this is Patty, David, Scott, Kelsey, Rob, Jenna, and Cole." He points to each as he repeats their names. "The little blonde is my big sister, Georgia, and that guy she's getting way too friendly with is Trey. And I think you know Bianca."

"Hi, it's nice to meet you," Patty says, stepping forward to shake my hand before wrapping her arms protectively around David, who gives me a quick wave. Patty's a blonde too, just as skinny and flawless looking as Georgia, in a pale blue tank top and white Capri jeans. David, by contrast, is bulky with dark hair and a nose with an odd ridge in the center.

"Don't worry, there's no test later or anything." Jenna smiles, her long, stringy, ginger hair hanging over her freckled shoulders as she begins digging through the box. Finally, she draws out two glass jars, thrusting them my direction. "Sweet or dill?"

I point to the dill spears, and she nods in agreement.

The only male not subtly being claimed by a girl is Cole. He leans against one of the four brick pillars at the corners of the pavilion, his legs crossed at the ankles. His blue V-neck T-shirt is stretched tight across his chest and biceps. It's the same shade as his eyes, which are the color of pool water, bright and stunning. I only realize I'm staring at him because he flashes me a smile that is twenty-percent friendly, eighty-percent this-guy-is-bad-news. It's probably meant to make me uncomfortable, but I just raise one eyebrow at him and smirk.

Scott waves the spatula at me from where he stands over the outdoor grill. He flips a few burger patties and drops a couple of hot dogs on with a hiss, the smell coming from it nothing short of heavenly.

"Hello." I wave shyly.

Oliver pats my shoulder, and then walks over to the grill to assist. I round the bench to where Bianca sits. "Hey," I say, squatting on the bench beside her, my back pressed against the tabletop.

She looks up, finally. "Oh, hey."

I sneak a peek at her computer. The screen is black except for a scroll of small, thumbnail-sized images and text streaming through the center of her screen. I recognize it quickly. It's an omega portal, part of the black net, an area of the web frequented by game designers—not a place most people even know exists, much less could access.

"Whatchya doing?" I ask curiously.

She closes the lid. "Homework."

Her face is void of emotion when she speaks, but there is arrogance in her tone.

"On an omega portal?" I ask, leaning away just a bit. "What's the assignment?"

She sits back, her dark eyes reluctantly impressed as she reaches up, adjusting her ponytail. "Psychology stuff. Did you know you can buy or sell anything on there? It's completely unregulated. I'm writing a paper about girls who sell their virginity online."

I feel my eyes widen. "Ugh. That's so disturbing."

I must look truly repulsed because she chuckles. "Don't worry, I'm not in the market to buy or sell."

From across the table, one of the guys, whose name I've already forgotten, chimes in. "Oh yeah, that ship sailed long ago."

She puckers her lips and flips him off. "Anyway, I'm writing a paper about deviant behavior in teen girls. What drives them to do things like that. I'm trying to contact some girls willing to talk about it."

I nod. It's a really interesting subject, actually. "Well, I'm pretty handy with a computer. If I can help at all..." I trail off, but she smiles.

"I'll let you know."

"Everybody, grab a plate. It's ready," Kelsey announces before I can say anything else.

If you've never had the opportunity to watch a group of teenage football players devour grilled meat, it's kind of like watching a school of piranhas take down an antelope. Ferocious, terrifying, and over quickly. Plus, anyone who gets between them and their food may end up with a bloody stump where their hand used to be.

I pick at the remnants of my cheeseburger and grocery-store potato salad. The spread, while simple, was still impressive; I've never met a group of people my age that could do more than order pizza without help. The soda is cold and brown, as it should be, when Cole passes it to me, cracking it open with a hiss before putting it in my hand. He sits to my left, Oliver on my right.

"So," Cole asks. "Suppose you've heard all the good Ferris Bueller jokes already."

I smirk. "Odds are good. Why... you got one?"

He sits back, looking serious. "Nah, I was trying to go with something about driving backwards, but I can't make it work. All I could come up with was, 'You wear too much eye makeup. My sister wears too much. People think she's a whore'."

"That makes you Charlie Sheen in this scenario?"

He smirks. "I'm Charlie Sheen in every scenario."

Shaking my head, I turn back to Oliver, who is passionately discussing the new James Bond movie. Most of the girls are picking at leafy green salads or hot dogs.

As if reading my mind, Cole leans over, whispering, "What is it with girls who eat like birds?"

I glance around. Not one of them is over a size six, I estimate, but by the way they are moving food around their plates and not ever really taking bites, you'd think they're counting calories or something. I stab a big chunk of potato and stuff it into my mouth unapologetically, making a face at Cole, who chuckles. Oliver stands up to toss his plate and soda in the nearby trash can, and Georgia slides into his empty place at my side.

"So, how are you liking CPHS so far?" she asks kindly, her voice light and singsongish.

I swallow the food in my mouth quickly, getting it wedged in my throat, forcing me to take a swallow of soda to wash it down. "Um, it's good so far. I'm not completely sucking at any of my classes, always a bonus, and I haven't gotten in a knife fight or anything. Yet," I add with a wry smile.

"I saw you at lunch sitting with those emo kids. I was afraid you were one of them," Jenna interjects haughtily.

For a second, I'm sure I've misheard her. But as I stare at her, my mouth hanging open just a fraction, she continues.

"I mean, not that there's anything wrong with them, I guess, but they don't really... I don't know. It's like they just hate everything. You seem nice. If you want, you can sit at our table from now on," she offers cheerfully.

Bianca perks up for the first time. "Don't be a brat, Jenna. They're really nice."

Jenna waves her off. "Please. You just hang with them because you have an unrequited girl crush on Cassy."

Georgia reaches out, smacking Jenna on the arm sharply. I glance over and see the warm flush rising to Bianca's cheeks, something clicking into place in my head. That's why the rest of us got the cold shoulder. Bianca is into Cassy. I can feel the awkwardness hanging in the air, a strange, unspoken stillness.

Trying to shift the focus off her, I shrug. "Can't blame her. Cassy's super cute. Sweet too."

Jenna swings her gaze to me, looking confused. "Are you into girls?"

I flick my hair back over my shoulder. "I'm straight, if that's what you mean. But I get it, is all I'm saying." I speak flippantly, as if I couldn't care less, and honestly, I couldn't.

Jenna's smile falters, replaced with a confused

frown. Beside me, Georgia lifts her soda can. "I agree."

"All the same, you're welcome at our table any time," Kelsey offers.

Georgia leans over and whispers in my ear, "Don't mind them. They're still getting used to having a lesbian on the squad. Plus, I think they share a handful of brain cells between them."

I laugh tensely. Hyenas, much like cheerleaders, are pack animals. If one of them smelled blood, they'd all move in for the kill.

"That Reid boy is cute though, in a nerdy, hipster kind of way. He helped me with a bio project last year. He was nice. Shy, but nice," Patty offers, her smile dazzling. Georgia visibly flinches at the mention of his name, but says nothing.

I nod. "He is nice. They all are."

It's then I realize all the guys have vanished from the table. I look around and see them getting ready to play a game of flag football in the park next to us.

I stand, toss my plate in the trash, and walk onto the grass to join the game. Oliver sees me approaching and waves me over.

"All right, guys, touch only. And the first person who smacks one of the girls on the ass gets to deal with me." He levels the threat through the huddle. At first, they chuckle, but then, realizing he isn't joking, they all nod.

We get off six plays, the last a long bomb from

Oliver to Cole. He breezes past me and I lunge for David, who is hot on his heels, managing to get both hands on his side before getting tripped up and falling to the ground. Looking up, I see Cole cheer, spiking the ball and shouting just before a bolt of lightning splits across the sky, which has darkened substantially without my noticing. Everyone looks up, waiting.

Less than three counts later, the thunder rolls, and the rain lets loose like a torrent from the sky. I feel a hand on my arm and realize Oliver is trying to help me to my feet. The freak rainstorm pours down on us as we bolt off the field and to the shelter of the pavilion, hitting the tin roof over the picnic area like nails.

"Well, I think the victory party is over," Oliver says, craning his neck to look at the sky. There's a bustle of movement as people clean up the tables, scraping the last of the food from the grill and filling the nearby trash can with garbage. With muttered farewells, they begin to disperse, ducking into the rain and running for their vehicles. Trey grabs Georgia, scooping her into his arms like a baby and running for it. She waves over his shoulder, and Oliver nods in her direction. Bianca tucks her computer in her oversized designer purse and scuttles for her celery-green Prius. Finally, there are only three of us left. Cole turns, offering Oliver a friendly fist bump.

"Later man," he says. Turning his attention to me, he jerks his chin upward. "Nice chatting with you Farris." Then, zipping his black hoodie and pulling it up over his head, he strides into the rain, walking slowly, deliberately, toward his black CRV.

Oliver waves as Cole pulls out of the parking lot, gravel spitting from his tires as he peels off, and then grabs me around the waist, pulling me close to his chest. The gesture is surprising, but not unwelcome. I'm soaked and cold and I can feel his body heat radiating off him like a furnace so I snuggle against him, trying not to shiver and failing.

He smells good in the rain. Spicy, like curry. Between us, I can feel his heart beating frantically, as if struggling to match speed with my own, which I can feel in my face. My head swims in the scent of him, his closeness, the feel of his arms around me. At first, I think he's going to kiss me. Our faces are so close, his eyes searching mine for something...

If he'd tried to kiss me then, I would have let him. The sound of the rain on the roof is hypnotic, lulling me into this mellow, calm place. He lifts his chin, resting it on the top of my head, so I tuck my nose into his chest. As we stand there, pressed together, I feel myself tingling, first in the tips of my fingers, then along my arms, and finally up my back into my neck. I'm not sure if I'm warming up or having some kind of episode. For the first time in what feels like forever, I take a breath, a clean, full breath that draws oxygen into the lowest parts of my lungs, and I feel completely at peace. Safe. Like the world can keep turning and everything can go back to normal.

I forgot how good it felt to just be held. As if somewhere, deep down, the damaged pieces of me are carefully sliding back into place.

I'm not sure how long we stand there like that, but the rain begins to slow, the patter of droplets on the roof growing soft. When he finally pulls back, just a little, he cups my face in his hands. I feel my fingers slide up his chest, across his red flannel shirt. When he lowers his face again, I rise up to meet him, our lips connecting in a sweet, chaste kiss.

And then another, less chaste kiss.

For a while, there's nothing else, just us, suspended in our own little bubble universe. Nothing else matters. I let myself drown in him, in the taste of his lips and the feel of his fingers in my hair, pausing only to catch my breath and start again.

By the time we head for his truck, hand in hand, my lips are swollen and tender from the kissing, a silly grin plastered to my face. This time when he starts the truck, he drapes his free hand on my knee, looking at me bashfully. I smile, covering his hand with my own.

We make it back, and I pull my cell from my pocket to check the time on my cell when the base alarms go off.

The sound paralyzes me, freezing the blood in

my veins.

"What is that?" Oliver mutters, glancing around.

The echoing wail of the sirens is part foghorn, part tornado-warning alarm, and all bad. It means something is happening, and it isn't something good. It can be anything from a terrorist attack to a plane crash to a biological weapon disbursement. There is simply no way to know.

"The base is locking down. Something's going on," I say. I haven't heard this sound since September eleventh, the day that terrorists had flown planes into the Twin Towers and the Pentagon. That was the first time I'd heard it, and hearing it again now, I can actually feel ice forming in my veins, cold and hard.

"What do we do?" he asks.

"Right now, all we can do is head to our houses and wait for news."

Oliver is surprisingly calm as he drives toward my house without another word. My knuckles are white as I cling to the handle over his passenger window. A dozen scenarios run through my mind on the short drive home. I cling to the hope that whatever is happening isn't happening here. That whatever's going on, my dad is safe.

When my phone goes off, the vibration nearly makes me jump out of my seat. It's playing U2's "Vertigo," my dad's ringtone. I answer quickly.

"Dad?" I ask, my voice an octave higher than

usual. "Are you alright?" I know better than to ask for details. No matter what's happening, he won't give details over the phone. And honestly, that's fine. Because he's calling. Which means he's alive. Which means I can breathe.

"Yeah, kid. It's me. Listen, go straight home and wait for me there. I don't know how long I'll be." His voice is tight, nervous, making unease bloom in my stomach.

I feel like I could cry, a strained mixture of relief and worry flooding my system. But I don't cry. That won't help anything. The Lieutenant Colonel has trained me well. We are clearly in some kind of emergency situation and instantly, like the flipping of a switch, I go into crisis mode.

"Yes, sir," I say, asking nothing else.

Click.

"Your dad okay?" Oliver asks softly.

I nod, my teeth grinding against each other too tightly to answer out loud. I just need to get home, to get everything together.

We come to a screeching stop in front of my house almost a minute before I realize we're there. My brain is too busy making plans, going over contingencies.

"Thanks for today, Oliver. I had a good time," I say earnestly.

He smiles. "Me, too. We should do it again. Like next weekend," he hedges.

I blink. There's something going on that weekend, I vaguely remember. It's fuzzy, hovering in the corner of my churning mind. Then it hits me. The brightly colored posters hanging around the school. Saturday after next is homecoming. I frown.

"Are you asking me to homecoming?" I ask, raising one eyebrow. "Geez. You make out with a guy for five minutes and he thinks you're an item."

I don't want him to hear the fear in my voice. Parties I can handle. Clubs? No problem. Sketchy raves? I'm in. But school dances are a little outside my wheelhouse. Mostly because I've never actually been to one.

"Yeah. The game is Friday, if you'd like to come watch me play, but I was referring to the dance Saturday."

Wow. Homecoming.

"Unless you're holding out for a better offer," he says with a wicked grin.

Okay. No pressure there.

"Dance. Wow. That implies things like dresses and corsages, right? I'm not sure..."

The truth is, I don't own anything more formal than the white cotton skirt I occasionally wear as a bathing suit cover-up at the beach.

He laughs. "You don't have to wear a dress if you don't want to. We'll both show up in holey jeans and wife-beaters. It'll start a whole new trend. Plus, while I've never gone to a homecoming dance myself, the movies imply there's a good chance there may be zombies."

I laugh, a little of the tightness slipping away, even as the sirens continue to ring out. "Well, I wouldn't want to miss the zombies," I say with a shrug. "Sure. Sounds fun."

He darts across the seat, kissing me quickly before I close my door and he speeds off.

The journey from the door of his truck to my front door is a blur. All I know is I'm still wet from the rain and hot from blushing. Gradually, my faculties return and my head clears. I walk to my living room, flipping my TV on to the local news. There's nothing being reported. Not a huge surprise, but a disappointment.

One might assume that, like the old adage, "no news is good news" in that sort of situation, but actually the opposite is true. When alarms are blaring on base and none of the local news stations are mentioning it, it means someone is being told to keep it quiet. *So it isn't a national incident,* I tell myself. Whatever had happened is only happening *here.*

Making a beeline for my bedroom, I pull a green duffel bag out from under my bed and toss it on top. I tug the zipper down and methodically examine the contents. One change of clothes—gray sweatpants, socks, underwear, and a T-shirt; a fully stocked first-aid kit; a SAT phone; a roll of money—

three hundred dollars cash, small bills; a credit card; a small black address book full of names and numbers of friends and relatives; a flashlight; two MRE main meals; a jug of water and finally, a bag of toiletries. The idea behind the emergency bag is that if the worst happens, it will be enough to get me somewhere safe. I repack the bag carefully, trying to keep the more important things near the top. I count and recount the cash before folding it over the credit card and twisting the rubber band around it, click the flashlight on and off to check the batteries, and hit the green button on the phone, checking to make sure it is working before turning it off again with a beep.

I really should keep this in the trunk of my car, I think. If I'd gotten locked off base, it would have been nice to have. Of course, it still wouldn't have done me much good today, seeing as I hadn't driven. That is an oversight I'm not likely to make again. I stuff the bag back under my bed and sit down on the edge of my frilly comforter, pulling my tablet out of my bag. Staring at it, I realize I could know exactly what was happening in a matter of minutes. I still have the paper with Dad's work IP address. It wouldn't take anything to hack in and take a peek. He'd never even know I was there. Staring at the still, dark screen, I think about it.

I've never considered myself a hacker. *Ability*, I tell myself, *does not mean intent*. I've never broken the law or created chaos for the sake of chaos. Hacking is all about ego. And that's one place where I'm not fucked up. Finally, with a deep sigh, I flip it on. Desperate to take my mind off the ticking minute hand of my alarm clock, I open my browser.

Realizing that with the base on lockdown, I'd never make it out this weekend to go get my new bedroom stuff, I decide on the next best thing. Online shopping. Generally, I'm not a fan, as it's so hard to pick stuff out without really seeing it and feeling it, but my options are slim. I wander site to site before settling on a sleek white bed set with a black paisley pattern. I find a couple of shiny black table lamps and matching curtains. The screen jumps to a writing desk that's white with black iron embellishments. *Why not?* I think, clicking on the purchase button.

From there, I browse a few gown places that have local outlets. I still can't believe I agreed to attend the warped social odyssey that is homecoming. With any luck, Oliver would be right and there'd be zombies. I can only hope.

Still unable to sit still any longer, I get up and roam the townhouse, wandering aimlessly in and out of rooms. When I flick the light on in the spare bedroom, I blink in surprise. I expected it to be full of storage boxes and Dad's junk, but it isn't. A sturdy oak desk sits in the middle of the room, a small antique metal lamp on one corner, a set of tall, wide monitors in the center, and a tiny desktop fridge on the other edge.

My throat constricted. Dad had done this for me, probably while I was out today. He set up this whole room so I'd have a place to work on my game design. My old computer had been damaged during packing; a careless mover dropped it and they'd had to cut us a check to replace it. I round the desk, looking at the computer. It is just like my old model, only two years newer. I hit the power button and the face lights up bright green.

Leaving only long enough to grab a cup of coffee from the kitchen, I sit down in the new, high-backed, cushioned rolling chair and slide myself up to the desk. I set to work installing my personally tweaked version of Linux, my preferred operating system, and stripping out all the random things that come pre-loaded on my hard drive. It takes several hours to get it exactly how I want it, a task that keeps me distracted and my brain occupied. Then, when all that is done, I retrieve all my software from my data cloud and begin the process of installing all that as well.

It's after eleven when Dad gets home. My fingers ache, my back stiff and protesting when I rise from my desk to greet him at the door. I don't remember the sirens stopping but at some point, they did. I wait, meeting him at the door, a cold beer in hand, which I quickly hold out to him. His proud shoulders slump as he shrugs out of his green jacket and hangs it on the wooden coat rack, taking the beer with a grateful smile. I step into him like I had when I was a little girl, throwing my arms around his broad shoulders and squeezing him as tightly as I can. He hugs me back, my feet leaving the floor before he sets me back down gently.

"What happened?" I ask.

"In there." He nods toward the living room.

I move to the living room sofa and sit down, bracing myself for bad news. *He's home*, I keep telling myself. How bad could it be?

He takes a seat in his favorite recliner and slowly unlaces his boots before sitting back, twisting open his beer, and taking a long drink.

"I got an in-flight discrepancy report today from one of the planes."

I sit back, sucking in a breath. "In English, please."

"When something goes wrong with one of the jets, the onboard computer sends a message to the maintenance department letting them know what the problem is, so they can fix it." He rubs the back of his neck. "We had thirteen flights go up today. They each sent the same error message."

I bite my lip. "What message?"

"Catastrophic engine failure."

I sit back. "All of them? Were they, I don't know, sabotaged or something?"

He shakes his head. "We pulled one of the engines apart. There's no issue we can find."

"So an error with the computers then?" I ask.

He nods, licking his lips. "There's more. I shouldn't even be telling you about it, but I figure you've got a right to know. Still, this stays between us, got it?"

I nod, so he continues. "The email I got from the plane wasn't a discrepancy. It was a warning. Someone manipulated the computers to send out false codes."

I blink rapidly, letting that sink in. Someone hacked the planes. I know all the systems in the JSF are automated, but this is unheard of. I don't ask how it happened. I could probably do it myself if I really tried. That in itself is a terrifying thought.

Seeing my expression, he leans forward, "So I have to ask..."

I cut him off. "I didn't do this," I say defensively.

He shakes his head. "No, I know it wasn't you. But you are one of the best computer people I know. You could probably code circles around those idiots they brought up to fix the computer issues. So if someone did do this, how do you think they did it?"

"How would I have done it, you mean?"

He nods.

I take a deep breath, releasing it slowly. "First, I'd need a way in. Your computers run on UNIX, and that's basically unhackable. But, some of the work station computers are dual OS, so I'd go in that way. I'd send a meme, something with an eagle and a flag, as a jpeg to one of those unprotected emails. Once they got opened, it would get sent to all the other Unix-based computers. I'd hide a virus or malware behind the jpeg."

He pulls his phone out of his pocket, opens up his email, and passes the phone to me. "Something like this?"

The image is exactly as I described. An eagle superimposed on a flag with a message that read, 'Freedom through superior firepower'. There were two crossed M-16s at the bottom. I nodded. "Yeah, something like this. Something they'd be likely to pass around."

"But we just cleaned out the systems," he says, taking the phone back. "Any viruses would have been cleared out."

I shrug. "Not if all the virus did was create a backdoor into the system, then delete itself. They wouldn't even be looking for it. But, having that on your phone, you should get it swept for malware, just to be safe."

He pinches the bridge of his nose and closes his eyes. "This is a fucking disaster."

"Why? If you know the messages were bogus, then what's the issue?"

He looks up. "The fleet is down for fourteen days, for testing. We can't fly again until they bring the DOJ in to confirm the error. We'll be lucky to be ready for the deployment in time."

"So why do you think this is happening?" I ask, wringing my hands together.

He scratches his head. "Whoever it is, they want to stop the deployment. There are a million reasons someone might want to do that. Which means I get to spend the next fourteen days talking to each department, trying to find someone who might know something about it, someone who has a reason to want to stay."

I let that sink in. He's right; there are a million reasons someone might want to blow a deployment. But if this is fixed soon enough, that person will have to escalate in order to get what they want. I shudder at the thought.

"I can help," I offer. "I can take a look at your computer, try to pick up a trail."

"I need you to stay clear of all this, ok?" he says sternly. "How would it look if the DOJ gets here and finds out that you, the CO's daughter, has been screwing around in the system? They might think you had something to do with it. I won't risk that."

"I can at least look at your phone for you, maybe see if that image has anything hidden inside?"

He thinks about it for a minute. "No. Not a good idea. Let us handle this," he says in a tone that tells me the conversation is over.

I curl my knees into my chest as he stands

and heads toward the kitchen. I'm still holding my sneakers when he yells, "You hungry? How 'bout frozen taquitos?"

"Pork?" I ask, straightening myself out.

"Of course."

"I'll have two," I holler, standing. If he honestly thinks that's the end of the conversation, he has a surprise coming.

Something strange is going on, and I'm going to find out what.

EIGHT

S UNDAY COMES AND GOES IN A BLUR OF FOOTBALL and homemade chili, Dad's favorite things. My ploy at softening him up has gone unnoticed, or at least, uncommented upon. Some weirdly protective button has been switched on in my brain, and I'm nagged by the desire to do something—anything— to fix the mess he found himself in. For his part, Dad seems pretty relaxed about it all. I suppose knowing the reason for the chaos has at least absolved him of the guilt that came from thinking it was his doing. Funny how having someone to blame, someone to point a finger at, could set one at ease. Even if that person is a nameless, faceless ghost in the machine.

I haven't asked him any more about it yet, though I've been twitchy with it, questions always on the tip of my tongue, but not wanting him to realize I'm not going to drop the matter as instructed. It'll be easier to snoop around if he doesn't know I'm still interested. It will also allow him some measure of plausible deniability if I'm caught.

Besides, he should really know better. I am one of those kids who shake their Christmas gifts to see if I can figure out what they are weeks before the event. Spending most of my down time curled on the couch with my tablet, I scroll through the social media accounts of some of his Marines, looking for the same thing he'll be looking for next week. A suspect. Someone with reason to want off the deployment cycle. Nothing is jumping out at me. By nature, soldiers aren't big on sharing personal stuff, especially online. Hours pass and my eyes sting, dry and raw from staring at the screen. I close them, pressing my thumb and forefinger on the lids until they water.

This is pointless. None of these people appear to have the means to perpetrate something like this. Ninety percent probably don't know the difference between an MD5 hash and a XOR function. I sigh, rolling my head side to side, stretching the stiff muscles.

Frustrated but trying not to let it show, I head back to my bedroom and lock myself away with a well-worn copy of *Beowulf*. I fall asleep on my floor reading.

When I wake up Monday, there's a tight knot in my back to match the one in my chest. I'd woken up just long enough to strip to my underwear before climbing into bed and crashing out again. Now, the sun is rising, its warm glow filling my room. Kicking off my blanket, I scuttle to the bathroom, showering and brushing my teeth as quickly as possible, trying to focus on the day ahead. In one weekend, I've gotten close to two great guys, who just happen to hate each other.

No, this isn't going to be awkward at all.

I wish, as I slide into a pair of dark denim jeans and a faded blue tank top, that there were some obvious flaw to one of them that would make it easier on me to simply choose one or the other. But that's not the case. I like them both, in different ways and for vastly different reasons. I want them both. Maybe that makes me selfish. I'm not sure I care. I just hope I can keep their drama off me, at least for as long as possible.

When I get to the kitchen, expecting to see Dad at the table, the room is empty. A yellow sticky note hangs from the fridge. I snatch it off quickly.

Kid,
I had to go to work early. Why don't you come by after school?
Love, Dad

I crumple the paper and toss it into the wire trash can as I grab the last of the still-warm coffee and pour myself a cup. Does he want me to come in and look at his computer? Has he changed his mind about wanting my advice? I let the thoughts roll around in my head. Finally, I go back to my room, rummaging around for the small, yellow firewire cable in my desk. Stuffing it and my tablet in my bag, I head for the door.

IN THE CAR, DEREK IS HIS USUAL QUIET SELF WHILE Kayla rattles on about the lockdown on Saturday. They had both been off base and were looking forward to a night in a hotel until the MPs had reopened the gate, ruining their plans. The only one who seems disturbed by the event is Reid. Of course, with his parents being in the squadron, he was probably as nervous as I'd been. His agitation shows clearly now, in the tight, square set of his jaw, the dark circles under his eyes.

I should have called him, I think, guilt gnawing at me. Things like that are always easier to handle in groups. I make a mental note to call him if, God forbid, it happens again.

The whole school is buzzing about the lockdown. Rumors fly like fire on the wind, everything from a plane crash to a bomb scare. No one seems to have it figured out, but everyone has a theory. I listen, nodding or making a shocked face when appropriate, pretending to be as clueless as the rest of them. Only a very stern lecture from my homeroom teacher manages to quell the rampant speculation and get everyone on task. After class, Oliver waits for me in the doorway with some of the boys I recognize from the picnic, Trey and Cole. Instead of walking off when they see me, they wait in a large group, smiling warmly in my direction.

Of course, these are the same boys I accused of being sacks of dicks not two weeks ago. I can't help but smirk a little at the memory.

"Hey Farris," Trey greets me with a jerk of his chin.

"'Sup, girl?" Cole asks, holding his fist out to me expectantly. I raise one eyebrow and he laughs, retracting it.

"Hi guys." I smile, trying not to look awkward.

Oliver snakes his arm around my shoulder and with one smooth movement, slips my backpack off my back and onto his. It's so 1950s, him carrying my books like that. The gesture makes me feel very girlie, and I'm not altogether sure how I feel about it.

It's not like I'm one of those girls who doesn't want her doors opened and for her date to pay for dinner. Those things are all very nice. Chivalry can be a beautiful thing. But this, it somehow triggers another part of my brain, the defiant, angry part that is fully capable of carrying her own books, thank you very much. While I struggle internally, trying to figure out my own stupid, emotional damage, Cole pipes up.

"So, you catch the game yesterday?" he asks. "The Panthers game, that is."

I nod. "Yeah, and thank God I did, because the refs clearly didn't."

He stops, waving his hand. "And did you see that block in the back in the third quarter?"

"I bet he's out all season. They say how bad it was yet? Looked like a blown ACL to me."

He nods, rubbing the back of his neck. "Yeah, man, that was ugly."

"I'm just glad they squeaked it out. That could have cost them the playoff spot," Trey adds. "What about you, Ollie? You catch the game?"

He shakes his head. "Nah. I had a project I had to work on all day."

"By project, you mean playing on your PS3, don't you?" Rob asks, his tone light, punching Oliver in the arm as he melds into the group.

We walk down the hall in a loud, boisterous group, continuing to talk football. Stopping occasionally, we pick up a couple of the girls, who quickly change the subject.

"What are you doing this weekend?" Jenna asks as she is hoisted onto Rob's back, monkey style.

"Um, well..." I pause.

Has Oliver told them about homecoming? Does he want me to say anything? I take a breath and go for it. "Oliver asked me to the dance," I say, trying to sound like it's no big deal.

"And you said yes?" Georgia asks slowly, arching one perfect eyebrow. "I figured you for smarter than that," she teases.

"Well, I tried to say no, but he wore me down," I say with a shrug.

She chuckles and pats me on the back. "Yeah. He's good at that."

When she sticks her tongue out at Oliver, he grabs her, roughly rubbing her head as she shrieks and tries to fix her hair.

The group breaks off and heads our separate ways, except for Oliver, who walks me to my next class before returning my backpack. Reid is leaning against the doorjamb, donut bag in hand. My heart falls to my feet as I watch his face darken.

"See ya at lunch," Oliver says, turning on his heel and stalking off.

Reid holds out a donut, his expression unreadable. "Thanks," I mutter, feeling like a total ass. He doesn't say anything, just turns and leaves.

Kayla is waiting for me by my desk.

"So, you and Oliver?" she asks.

"Maybe," I say noncommittally.

"And Reid?" she asks sharply. "You know they can't stand each other."

I lean in, lowering my voice. "I know. But does that mean I can't be friends with both of them? Do I really have to choose?"

She folds her arms across her chest. "Historically, yes."

"That doesn't seem fair." I frown. "I don't know

what to do."

She smiles, her dark purple lipstick thinning as it presses against her white teeth. "You want my advice?"

Do I? Probably not. "Sure."

"This school runs on a system of cliques and balances. No matter how much you want to be neutral, it won't stay that way. It's like, an unwritten rule. You'll end up swinging this way or that, and before you know it, you've chosen a side without ever meaning to. It happens; I've seen it."

I shake my head. "And if I refuse to choose? If I decide I want to cross the lines, break the rules?"

She flicks her long, black fingernail. "Then a side will be chosen for you."

I KNOW OLIVER EXPECTS ME TO JOIN HIS TABLE FOR lunch, which leaves me with a problem. After my valiant speech about not allowing myself to be drawn into one clique or another, here I am, being pulled away from Kayla and Derek and the rest of my little group. The whole thing is making me so ill I may not be able to eat anyway. I don't want Reid and the others to think I'm ditching them, but I also don't want to blow off Oliver. I nibble on my thumbnail as I wait for Reid by his locker after class.

"Hey, Reid. You got a sec?" I ask.

He reaches past me, opening his locker and

tossing a book inside, then slams it quickly. "Sure, what's up?"

We walk toward the cafeteria, but I keep my pace slow.

"I got invited to sit with Oliver today, and I don't want you to think it's a permanent change, or because I don't like you." I fidget with the strap of my bag, realizing how stupid and childish I sound. "I don't want to be stuck in one clique. I don't want to have to take sides or get drawn into a fight between you. I want to hang out with both of you. And I don't want it to be a problem."

His face twitches in my peripheral vision. "You've been talking to Kayla." I don't say anything, but it isn't really a question anyway. Finally, he stops walking, turning to face me, "Look, I get it. I get that you don't want to wade into someone else's drama. So, if you want to be friends with both of us, well, that's your choice. Just don't expect the three of us to go get coffee together. Because that's never gonna happen."

"So you're saying I can be friends with both of you, just not at the same time?" I ask.

He nods. "That's the deal."

"Fair enough," I say, raising my hands in surrender.

He jerks his head, and we start walking again. "Has he asked you to homecoming yet?" he asks, a twinge of something in his voice I can't quite place.

"Um, yeah. I said yes."

He licks his bottom lip just a little. "How 'bout you and I go see a movie tonight? Since your weekend is taken." He laughs, and there's an edge to it.

"I'd like that. But I'm going to eat with him today," I say. "Don't worry, Cassy will be there to keep you company," I offer, wagging my eyebrows suggestively.

He blushes. "Have fun."

Guilt stabs at me. "Hey, I really appreciate you understanding."

"Well, I'm a truly remarkable guy. Just so you know," he jokes, nudging me in the side with his elbow. "But seriously, just be careful about Oliver. I don't know what he's into, but I know that if he hurts you, it'll be more than a few nasty words we exchange."

He steps in front of me, his adorable glasses slipping down his nose. His expression is serious, unwavering, a fierce protectiveness flashing behind his green eyes as he pushes his glasses back up. Stepping forward, he holds the door open for me, then gives me a goodbye wave as he heads to our usual table, leaving me standing there, death gripping my bag.

My eyes follow him to our table, where Derek and Kayla sit listening to music on her phone while they share a tray of chicken nuggets and fries. Glancing in the opposite direction, I catch sight of Oliver. He watches me with subtle interest as I make my way through the à la carte line, grabbing a chili dog and root beer. When I walk toward his table, I throw a wink at Kayla as I pass. Seeing me approaching, Oliver smacks Cole in the shoulder and gestures for him to scoot down. Cole slides over, making an empty space beside Oliver, and pats the seat before turning back to his conversation. I set my tray down and climb onto the bench.

Everyone talks over each other. Struggling to make sense of the chatter, I catch snatches of conversation about the weekend, the weather, dress shopping and, of course, the lockdown.

Oliver frowns, leaning into my side as he speaks. "Your dad alright?" he asks, his voice soft.

I nod.

"Any idea what happened?" he continues, taking a sip of his soda.

I make a pained face. "Not really. Only that no one was hurt."

"My mom says the fleet's grounded for two weeks. Some kind of system error they think." Bianca's voice rings out, louder than the others. She's picking at a grilled cheese, taking tiny, rolled-up bites.

"I didn't know your mom is in the squadron," I say, surprised.

She nods. "She's admin. Almost got in a hell of a lot of trouble when the ordering went all weird too. Turns out, it's a glitch or something."

In the back of my head, alarms go off, an internal

warning system I've learned to listen to over the years. Maybe Dad isn't looking for a Marine or even a spouse who wants to stop the deployment.

Maybe it's one of us.

"You wanna go with us?" Georgia asks in my direction, jarring me from my thoughts.

I shake my head. "Sorry, I must have zoned out for a minute. What was the question?"

Smiling slyly, Georgia repeats herself, her blond hair cascading over one shoulder like a silk curtain as she tilts her head my direction. "Do you want to go dress shopping with us tonight? For the dance?"

Oh. My brain stutters. "Um, actually I'm going with Kayla tomorrow night. But thanks for the invite," I say, smiling.

That isn't entirely true, but I'm betting she'll go with me.

"Kayla?" Patty asks.

"Yeah. My friend," I say, waving in Kayla's direction. She waves back, smiling through her eggplant-purple lipstick.

"Oh."

The girls mostly ignore me after that, even Georgia giving me an apologetic smile. They chew their tiny salads while I enjoy my chili dog. It's messy and delicious, and the girls are giving me strange looks. Finally, I turn to Oliver and whisper, "Do I have something on my face?"

He grabs a napkin and wipes a drip of chili off

my chin. "There, you're perfect," he says.

I grin like an idiot. Can't help it. That stupid dimple appears again and I'm down another ten IQ points.

Cole, however, is chatting with me like I'm one of the guys, never once trying to explain something he thinks I might not get, on account of being a girl and all. My gratitude toward him swells. We talk cars, and he and David listen intently as I talk about rebuilding the Mustang.

I glance at the other table from time to time, catching sight of my other friends laughing and talking. I wish I could merge the two groups, but I know that with the boys at odds, that will never happen. Soon, the conversation turns back to the dance and Trey starts complaining about the hassle of renting a tux.

"We can't all pull off double-oh-seven," David cracks.

"Speak for yourself," Cole cuts in.

"Not to burst any bubbles, but," Oliver smirks slyly, "I may be going to homecoming in jeans."

The guys laugh. The girls gasp in abject horror. They swing a glance from Oliver to me in disbelief. I hold up a French fry, smothered in ketchup.

"It's hard to get zombie goo out of silk," I say, stuffing it in my mouth before washing it down with my soda.

REID GETS TO CHEMISTRY LATE, SLIDING INTO THE seat next to me. He's flushed and breathing hard.

"Where'd you run off to?" I ask under my breath as the overhead projector flicks on, revealing the day's notes.

"I wanted to get you something," he answers quietly, leaning in to me. He slides a brown folder across the table. It has Oliver's name on it.

Frowning, I open my mouth to chastise him when the teacher starts talking, not too subtly looking my direction. My mouth closes with a snap, and I tuck the folder into my bag.

Reid slides his notebook in front of me.

Figured you should know the whole story.

I scribble a response.

Not cool. Would you want him passing out your personal file?

He sits back, looking petulant for a few minutes before writing something else.

Sorry. Didn't think of it that way. Just worried for you.

I shake my head again. Then something dawns on me.

How did you get this?

He writes back quickly.

Office aid third period. Sorry for overstepping. We still on for that movie?

Glancing up, I see him looking at me with his

bottom lip jutting out, his chin down and eyes wide. He clasps his hands together in a begging gesture. Smirking, I scribble back again.

Sure. I have to go to my dad's office first. You wanna come with?

I slide the notebook back across the table. The teacher claps once, telling us to begin. He lights the burner we share, the small, blue flame jumping to life between us. He glances at the page, and then folds it over.

"I should probably go home first, chores to do and stuff," he whispers, pouring a clear liquid into the warming test tube.

Behind us, I can hear Oliver tapping his pencil impatiently on his table. I peek over my shoulder and he winks at me. Shaking my head, I turn my attention back to the experiment and don't look back again until the bell rings.

As Reid gathers up his books, I scoop up the empty beakers and head for the sink at the back of the classroom. "You go ahead. I'll catch up," I say.

Reid frowns, but he nods and walks out. Oliver leans against the sink when I arrive to drop off the vials.

"Hey, Oliver, I need to talk to you for a second," I say as everyone else clears out. "I told Reid this, and now I'm telling you. I get that you guys aren't friends. But he's my friend, and I don't want to be put in the middle of your drama. Can you handle that?"

He takes a deep breath. "I really like you, Farris. You aren't like the other girls I know," he says, folding his arms across his chest. "But Reid is a problem for me. It makes me uncomfortable, the thought of you hanging out with him."

"You're going to finish that sentence with, but I will respect your decision, right?"

He licks his lips.

"Because it is my decision," I say before he can speak again. "I can't be with someone who tries to tell me who I can and can't be friends with. I won't be controlled like that. I need to know that you respect me enough to respect my choices."

And it's as simple as that. If his chivalry passes into the borders of being controlling, I'll drop him in a New York minute. Dimple or no dimple.

"He knows you're going to homecoming with me, right?"

"Of course."

"I don't feel good about it, but..." He rakes his hand through his hair. "God, why can't you be as boring as the others girls?"

That takes me back, and I make a sour face. "What's that supposed to mean?"

"It means, if I didn't like you so much, it probably wouldn't bug me so badly. But I do. I like you a lot. And I don't want to lose you over this. So yeah, I respect your decision. I don't like it, but I respect it."

Reaching out, he puts his hand on the back of

my neck, drawing me to him gently, before pressing his lips to mine. When he pulls back, his expression is pained. "Just watch out for him." His voice is shaky, like he's barely able to control it.

I roll my eyes. "Funny, he said the same thing about you."

He grunts. "See you tomorrow, Farris." Leaning forward he places another quick kiss on my mouth, making my lips burn and my chest tighten.

"Bye," I say, turning on my heel and walking away. I spare a glance over my shoulder before I step out of the doorway. "And Oliver? Thanks."

He nods, licking his bottom lip, looking pensive.

NINE

T<small>O SAY THAT</small> K<small>AYLA IS SURPRISED BY MY INVITATION</small> to go dress shopping would be an understatement. Her eyes go wide, her pale cheeks flush, and I realize that I may not be the only one attending a dance for the first time.

Despite the ever-present zombie threat, I have to admit I'm a little excited to do a formal dress-up thing. Though I'll never admit it out loud, the idea of doing the slow-motion walk down the stairs to greet my date, who would be dumbstruck by my beauty, hits all the girlie places deep inside me. For that, I blame John Hughes and his string of wildly cheesy 1980's movies playing in an endless cycle on cable TV.

Kayla agrees eagerly, touting her own need to find a gown. Apparently, black taffeta is hard to find. She suggests a trip to Charlotte the following afternoon and I'm immediately on board. Not only will the getaway be nice, but it'll give me a chance to ask her about Bianca, who is the only person besides myself I know to be capable of the hack that took down the squadron.

"We can leave after school and make an evening of it," she suggests.

"Sounds great. I just have to clear it with my dad," I say, dropping her and Derek off at her place.

"See if you can find me a black ascot while you're out, okay?" Derek says before they are out of earshot.

At first, I think he's joking, but then, maybe not. I wonder what his idea of Goth formal would look like and I snicker to myself, betting he'll show up looking like Gary Oldman in *Dracula*.

Grabbing my cell from my pocket before I pull away, I dial Oliver.

"Hello?" he answers, winded.

I wonder what he was doing. Surely practice hasn't started yet? "Hey, it's Farris."

He sounds surprised. "Oh. Hey. Didn't recognize your number. What's up?"

"Are you running?" I ask, checking over my shoulder as I pull out onto the street.

"Forgot my notebook in the classroom. Had to run back for it before practice. And now I'm heading to the gym."

"Oh. I was actually looking for Georgia. Can I get her number?"

"Uh, yeah. Actually, wait. She's right here; I'll just give her to you."

"Hello?" Her sweet voice cracks through the

speaker.

"Hey, it's Farris. So, Kayla and I are going dress shopping in Raleigh tomorrow after school and I was wondering if you wanted to go? I know you're going with your other friends already, but..."

I bite my lip. Truthfully, I have no experience with the whole dress-shopping thing and I need someone there who will know what to choose. If I just go with Kayla, I'll have fun, but I'll probably end up looking like a burlesque pinup girl. Plus, this might be a good opportunity to begin merging my friend groups, breaking through those social barriers.

"Yeah, that sounds like fun. I'll probably get my dress tonight, but I could help you pick something out," she offers.

"Great, we'll leave right from the school, okay?"

"Sounds good."

"Um, okay, thanks. Bye," I say.

"Bye."

I hold the phone to my ear a moment longer, just to see if she's going to hand it back to Oliver.

Click.

Apparently not.

A few minutes later, I pull into the parking lot at Dad's office. After parking, I make my way to his building, scanning my ID to get me through the tall, cylindrical turnstile. I find my way to his office without getting lost this time—point for me. The halls buzz like a beehive with activity. Dad's admin clerk is at her desk, shuffling papers with one hand and balancing a coffee cup in the other. My dad always jokes that's a required skill for promotion if you are an admin clerk. She's plump, but not fat, with dark red curls escaping from her tight bun. The plate on her desk reads: S1 Belford. So not Bianca's mom, but another of the pool of admin clerks attached to the squadron.

I walk past her, her eyes narrowing as they follow my every move, and tap on my father's door.

"Just a second," he calls out.

From behind the frosted glass, I see he's on the phone. Leaning against the door frame, trying to look nonchalant under the redhead's watchful eyes, I strain to listen at the crack.

"There was no evidence of a physical breach. Yes, all major workstations have been cleared, and we've upped gate personnel. Yes. They say the email originated from here on base. Just a prank, we think, but we're looking into it. Yes, sir."

I hear him put the phone down and push himself away from the desk, the wheels of his chair rolling across the wood floor.

"Come on in, kid," he calls, opening the door, and then closing it behind us.

"Hey, Daddy. How's it going?" I ask, taking a seat on the edge of his desk.

He flinches. "Uh-oh. The last time you called me

Daddy, we almost ended up with a pony. What do you want?" He leans back in his chair, hands behind his head, eyes narrowed.

"See, there's this dance, and well... I got asked to homecoming and I need to get a dress," I blurt out. Truthfully, it's only part of the reason for my visit. But I'll get to the rest after.

His face turns a delicate shade of purple as he lurches forward, nearly losing control of his rolling chair before recovering himself. "Who's the lucky boy?" he manages.

"Oliver," I say. "You've been introduced, remember?"

I still haven't forgotten his earlier comment about Oliver, but I'm determined to try.

Dad rolls his eyes. "Of course."

Then he flushes, dropping his eyes to the paperwork in front of him. "Do you need me to go shopping with you, or...?"

I practically jump off the edge of the desk. "No, no. No. I just need permission to use the credit card again. Some girlfriends and I are going to Raleigh after school tomorrow to find something."

The relief in his face is immediate. I imagine it's similar to the look someone has when getting out of prison.

He makes a shooing motion with his hands, "Sure, sure. Whatever you need, kid. Just uh, you know, don't uh, I mean, get something... appropriate."

I laugh out loud. What does he expect? For me to show up to homecoming in a string bikini?

I blink. "But, I was going to look for a dress down at the used stripper emporium. You know, save a little cash." He sighs deeply at my sarcasm. I hold up one hand. "Fine, I promise. Now what's all this?" I wave my hand over the stacks of papers strewn about his desk.

"Oh, the usual, orders to sign, leave requests to review, nothing interesting."

But I do see something interesting. Hanging off the corner of his desk is an email printout written in big, red letters. I have a pretty good idea what it is. And I need to get my hands on it.

Hmmm.

I walk around the desk to look at the pictures on the wall behind Dad's chair.

"What's this one?" I point to the highest one, a photo of three Marines standing next to an F-14.

Dad stands to get closer to the picture. As he steps forward, I step back, slipping the paper from the stack, behind my back, and stuffing it up the back of my shirt with a speed and silence born of years of practice. It is how I used to smuggle candy bars into Mom's hospital room.

"Oh, that's me and Rick and Lenny in Guam, back before you were born. Good times," he says, lost in some memory.

I bite my lip, rethinking telling him about my

suspicions. I'd rather take a look at the email first, see if I can confirm my theory. "Cool, well, I should get home. Homework and all that. Oh, and I might hit a movie later."

Dad is still staring at the picture, lost in thought. "Oh, okay. Just be home by eleven, kid."

"No problem. See you later, Dad." I stretch up on my tiptoes, giving him a quick peck on the cheek and slipping out the door before he turns around.

The clerk isn't at her desk when the door closes behind me, so I pull out the email, fold it quickly, and tuck it into my messenger bag before heading to my car.

Finally, I have something to go on.

I'M LOOKING OVER THE EMAIL AT THE KITCHEN TABLE when my cell phone rings. It isn't a number I recognize, but it could have been anyone here; I still don't have many of my new friends programmed into the memory. The only reason Oliver is in my contacts is because he'd done it himself on the second day of school.

"Hello," I answer.

"Hey, Farris. It's Reid."

"Oh, hey Reid. What's up?"

"I was just wondering if you have any idea of what you want to see tonight?"

I hadn't even thought about it. I feel a pang of

guilt. Putting down the printout I'd been staring at for the last hour, I rub my eyes. "Well, that new *Bullet Games* movie looks good. How about that?"

"Great. Pick you up in fifteen minutes?"

"Um, on the scooter?"

"There's room for two. Why? Not sexy enough for you?" He chuckles.

"Oh, I'm just being anal. I don't like to be off base without my car, in case anything happens."

He doesn't complain. It is quickly becoming one of my favorite things about Reid. "No problem. I'll just meet you at the theater."

"Thanks. See you soon."

I hang up, my attention drifting back to the email. If it was sent from the school computer lab, the time stamp will at least give me an idea of my suspects. I'll just pop in on the class and see who is there that hour. It isn't much, but it is a place to start.

THE MOVIE THEATER FEELS CRAMPED, DESPITE there only being a handful of patrons inside, and smells of stale popcorn. The seats are small and nestled close together, threadbare and probably at least three decades old. Reid shows up in a Birdhouse skater T-shirt and Vans shoes, a black knit cap slouched half off the back of his head. As soon as I see him, I smile. If he's going for skater-boy chic, he pulls it off. He looks like he should be playing in a garage band or something. He flops into the seat next to me.

"Hey, what's a nice girl like you doing in a place like this?" he asks.

"Eating my weight in popcorn and thin mints."

He chuckles, grabbing a handful of snacks.

When the lights go down, I become hyperaware of him in the seat next to me. Where Oliver makes me feel off-balance, Reid makes me feel solid, like the ground is firm beneath my feet. I stuff my mouth with popcorn, focusing on the movie that's just begun playing.

"How's your dad?" he asks, whispering the words into my hair as he leans over for another handful of popcorn.

My chest tightens, I'm not sure if it's the email, still tucked in the bag at my feet, or the smell of him, the heat of his breath on my ear, but my heart picks up speed and I can feel it under my ribs. "He's fine. Just trying to get things taken care of."

"Shhh!" someone a few rows back hisses. I sink further down into my seat.

"Yeah, my parents are freaked out. They're saying they might have to pull the deployment."

I lick my lips, the salt drying out my mouth so much I have to grab my soda and take a long slurp through the straw before answering. "No, Dad thinks they will have things fixed before then."

He nods. "That's good at least."

"Shhh!" the voice hisses again. I turn and toss a handful of popcorn at my shusher.

After about thirty minutes, I realize why there are so few of us in the theater. The flick, billed as a shoot-em-up action film, is horrifically, hilariously cheesy.

"This is terrible. You wanna bug out early?" he asks, as if reading my mind.

"God yes," I whisper back, relief thick in my voice.

As we slink out, I pause to get a look at the guy behind me, who I'd tossed the popcorn at. Cole waves at me from under a white baseball hat, his expression smug and playful. I shake my head and follow Reid out the doors, wondering if Cole being there is a coincidence, or if he is keeping an eye on me for his friend.

Bursting from the theater into the cool night air, Reid and I jog across the street to a small playground. Dropping my bag at my feet, I hop, standing, onto a swing and spin so the chains twist and untwist, making my hair fly back and forth as I move. Reid sits in the swing next to mine, his sneakers digging into the loose gravel.

"You seemed preoccupied in the theater. What's on your mind?" he asks with his face turned to the sky.

I stop spinning long enough to stare at him for a minute. Never in my entire life has someone just instinctively got me like Reid. I press my lips together in a line, debating what to say. I know Dad told me not to share the info he'd given me, but at the end of the day, if my theory is right, an ally— someone to help me do some digging—would really be nice.

"I'm sort of poking around into what happened at the squadron," I answer.

Whatever he'd expected me to say, it isn't that. He swings to a stop, his face serious. "What? Why? Aren't the authorities looking into it?"

I let myself slide down until I'm sitting in the swing, and then turn to face him, letting myself lean forward over my feet. "Yeah, but I... I think they are looking in the wrong place."

He frowns. "What do you mean?"

I swallow, drawing circles with the toe of my shoe. "The squadron started having system glitches. At first, it was small stuff, then, not such small stuff." I pause. "You have to keep this just between us, ok?" He nods, so I continue. "Someone hacked the onboard relay. Sent false error messages to the base computers. Again, they thought it was a glitch, until they got this."

I reach down, pulling the email out of my bag and unfolding it slowly, handing it to him.

He reads it, frowning. In large, red letters it reads:

Next time, it will be for real.

He passes it back to me. "Do they have any idea who's behind it?" he asks.

"Not yet. They are investigating, talking to all the active duty personnel. But the thing is, I don't think that's who's doing it."

"What's your theory?"

I think about it for a moment before answering. "What if it's one of us? One of the kids whose parents are in the squadron? We have as much reason as anyone else not to want the deployment to happen. And not to brag, but my dad can't even program the Blu-ray player. I bet most of the others are the same."

He looks down, biting at his bottom lip. "Yeah, that does make sense."

"My concern is that they're so buys looking in the wrong place..." I trail off, but he knows where I'm heading.

"That something serious will happen before they start looking in the right one."

I nod. "If this person's goal is to ground the fleet, when it goes back up in a week, they are gonna have to escalate to be taken seriously. And that means people getting hurt. And both of our parents," I gesture between us, "are in that line of fire."

He pauses, and then slowly asks, "So what's your play?"

I kick the rocks under my sneakers. "I'm going to use the timestamp on the email to try to back trace the IP. It will mean going through my dad's work email. He won't be happy about it if he finds out."

"What can I do?" he asks.

"Now that you mention it, I'd like to pull the files on any students with parents in the squadron."

He frowns. "Not the hard copies. One, you'd have to go through each manually, which would take forever, and plus, someone would probably notice that many missing files.

"Can you get me alone with one of their computers?"

He shakes his head. "The student files are on the guidance server. It's a closed network. You'd have to plug into one of them directly."

"I can handle that, with a little help from my friends."

He smirks.

"Also, what do you know about Bianca?" I ask, not looking at him.

"Not much. She's quiet, nice enough. She's Cassy's best friend. A cheerleader for the past two years or so. Good grades, I think. She asked me to tutor her and Cassy for a while, but I don't think she really needed it. Why, she a suspect?"

I stand, releasing the chains. "Honestly, I'm not sure just yet."

Taking the cue, he stands too, looking down at his watch. "Only nine thirty. You wanna go grab a coffee before we head home?" he asks.

I grab my bag. "That sounds really bad for me, coffee this late. It might stunt my growth."

He shrugs. "Maybe, but if I'm going to do one stupid thing tonight, it should probably be coffee, because if I sit here with you any longer, I'm going to do something even stupider. Like kiss you."

His admission catches me off guard. In two long strides, he's in front of me, grabbing the metal chains of my swing on either side. The world around me slows to a crawl as he leans forward. My breath hitches in my chest, and I freeze. Slowly, he presses his forehead against mine, his eyes focused on my mouth. I can feel him struggling with himself, the restraint knotting in his arm muscles. Finally, quickly, he kisses the top of my head gently and backs away. The world rushes back in so quickly I think I might collapse from the influx.

"Sorry," he says, shaking his head. "Shouldn't have done that."

I open my mouth to say something, but nothing comes out. What can I say? Do I even want him to kiss me? Would I have stopped him? I have no idea.

He holds his hand out. "Come on, Let's get that coffee."

1 1 0 1 0 0 0 1 1 0 0 0 1 0 1 1
0 0 1 0 1 1 1 0 0 1 1 1 0 1 0 0
1 1 0 1 0 0 0 1 1 0 0 0 1 0 1 1
0 1 0 1 1 1 0 0 1 1 1 0 1 0 0
1 0 1 0 0 0 1 1 0 0 0 1 0 1 1
0 0 0 0 0 0 0 0 0 0 0 0 0 0 0
0 1 0 1 1 1 0 0 1 1 1 0 1 0 0
1 1 1 1 1 1 1 1 1 1 1 1 1 1
0 1 0 0 0 1 0 0 **TEN** 1 0
0 1 0 1 1 1 0 1 0 1
1 1 1 1 1 1 1 1
0 1 0 0 0 1 0 0 0
0 0 0 0 0 0 0 0
1 1 1 1 1 1
0 0 1 1 0 1
0 0 1 1 0 1
1 1 0 1
1 1 0 1
0 0

O LIVER ISN'T AT SCHOOL THE NEXT DAY, BUT STAYS home sick, according to Georgia, who hands me a note before first period.

Farris,

Don't think this means you are getting out of homecoming. See you at the game, if not before. Have fun with Georgia today. Remember, jeans are still an option.

—Ollie

I smile and tuck the note into my backpack.

In the cafeteria, Reid slides me a list of names. "Behold, all the students with family in or attached to the squadron. That's the best I can do."

"I could kiss you," I say without thinking. Then my head jerks up, my words finally passing through my brain.

He smirks. "Relax. We're cool."

Looking over the list, my eyes stick on two

familiar names. Oliver and Georgia Knight.

"Why are Oliver and Georgia on here? I thought their dad was a doc?"

Reid responds after taking a sip of soda. "He's the squadron doc. He embeds with the troops when they deploy."

I frown, my gut rolling at the idea of him doing something like this. Is he even capable?

"Anything jump out at you?" Reid asks, taking another long draught of his soda.

Truth is, the name I'm most interested in just happens to be on the top of the page. Bianca Withers. I rub the back of my neck, not wanting to say anything out loud. Bianca is back with the cheerleaders today, but Cassy is sitting next to Reid, her expression pleasantly neutral as she stabs at her salad. I shake my head. "No one jumps out. You know these people better than I do; what do you think?" I hand the page back to him.

He glances over it, opening his mouth and then closing it quickly, catching my eye over the top of the page before handing it back. One corner of his mouth twitches, his eyes sliding across the room to Bianca and then back to me. I nod as subtly as possible. We really need her full file, and the others too, if we can manage it. Ollie's file is still sitting in my backpack like a guilty secret.

"Nothing, really. Now what?" he asks.

I tap my pencil on my chin, debating. "First, some

research, then a trip to the guidance counselor," I decide, lifting my water bottle to my lips.

He tilts his head quizzically. "You need a little guidance?"

He knows full well what I need, and his tone is teasing. "Oh, I think I'm always in need of some guidance," I say. "But what I could really use is a distraction. You up for it?"

The smile on his face is answer enough.

AFTER SCHOOL, KAYLA IS ALREADY WAITING NEAR MY car when Georgia and I arrive. She leans lightly on the hood, an offense for which I would have shot anyone else.

Full of nervous energy, I begin chatting. First introducing them, which is awkward and unnecessary, then droning on about the terrible movie I'd seen with Reid, all the while terrified that having Kayla and Georgia in the same car will be like mixing oil and water.

When I finally stop to take a breath, they fall into a light discussion about the latest celebrity gossip and converse the whole way. By the time we get there, they are laughing like they've been friends for years. Georgia, I realize, is one of those people you just automatically love. She has an amazing way of putting you at ease, making you feel welcome. It's the same charisma her brother has, and it's just as impossible to resist.

The mall is seriously picked over as far as formals go, so we head downtown to some specialty shops Kayla recommends. Less than an hour later, she has a lime-green-and-black dress with a short, tutu-like skirt and corset top. It looks great on her, even if it does make her look like some kind of morbid ballerina. I find a long, black gown with an empire waist and shimmery red vines lacing their way up the skirt. I pick up a red-and-black choker and matching earrings that graze my shoulders. Georgia declares the outfit perfect, and that's good enough for me.

I only hope Dad likes it as much, because the credit card is still smoking when I stuff it back into my wallet.

After a quick dinner at a place called Machas, which boasts a live mariachi band, we are back on the road home. Exhausted, we mostly just listen to the radio, occasionally congratulating ourselves on our amazing finds or bursting into song and wiggling in our seats to the beat.

I drop Kayla off first. Secretly, I'm hoping to get inside Georgia's house to check on Oliver. As I hoped she would, Georgia invites me in.

The floor plan of their house is almost exactly the same as Reid's, but the decor is vastly different. Oliver's parents have a bit of a flair for the dramatic that comes through in their expensive Victorian furniture and large, bold paintings. Also, as some long-timers do, they've repainted the rooms in contrasting color palettes that gives the whole house a warmer, more lived-in feel.

"I assume you'd like to check on my brother," Georgia says at the end of the tour.

I blush. "Am I that obvious?"

She just smiles and points to a closed door at the end of the hallway. "I'm going to go grab a snack," she says, gliding off to the kitchen.

I creep down the hall, my feet making no noise on the carpeted floor. Before I reach Oliver's room, a sound makes me pause, turning my head. Light is streaming through a half-open door of the bathroom to my left. I catch a glimpse of Oliver through the gap. I want to say something, to announce myself, but I don't, and I'm not sure why. But I just watch in the reflection of the mirror as he pulls an orange prescription bottle out of a drawer and snaps open the cap. He tosses two white pills into his mouth, washing them down with a deep drink of tap water. Slowly, quietly, I take a few steps backward. When he emerges, he's wearing a white T-shirt and boxers. I must have been holding my breath because little black spots swim in front of my eyes.

Oblivious to my presence, he closes himself back into his room. I slide into the bathroom, closing the door behind me.

Please God, be antibiotics.

As quietly as possible, sure the sound of the drawer rolling open will give me away, I dig through the random toiletries until I find the prescription bottle. The label has been meticulously peeled off. I pop off the cap and shake a few pills into my hand. They look innocuous, but hell, how am I supposed to know? All I know is they're round, white, and look just like aspirin except for the numbers 54-452 etched onto their surface. Snapping a photo with my phone, I return the pills to the tube and the tube to the drawer. I flush the toilet and run some water in the sink, leaning against the edge of the counter and staring at myself in the mirror for a few seconds.

Don't jump to conclusions, I warn myself. It could be anything, could be nothing. But I feel the wary edge of distrust creeping in, like a slick of oil over my skin. Finally, I splash a little water on my face, which I've watched grow pale in the reflection, and then dry off before making my way to Oliver's room, tapping gently on his door.

"Go away," he shouts from the other side.

I take an involuntary step back, stunned at the tone of his voice. It sounds so *cold*. I take another step back, wondering if I should just leave, and bump right into Georgia. She gives me a *don't mind him* expression and bangs on his door.

"Oliver, Farris is here," she hollers into the room.

When the door swings open, he's wearing jeans, to my relief and disappointment. I may have had a hard time talking to him in his underwear. The tension between us is thick enough without the lack of clothing.

"Um, hey," I say weakly. "I wanted to see how you were feeling."

He runs his fingers through his tousled hair, rubbing his head. "Oh. Yeah. I'm all right. Better. Come on in."

I step into his room as he grabs a pile of dirty laundry off his floor and tosses it into his hamper.

"Excuse the mess," he says, flopping himself onto his bed.

I shrug, stepping inside. "I'm glad you're feeling better. You gonna be at school tomorrow?" I ask.

His room is that of a typical guy. There's a surfboard-shaped corkboard, flyers for various bands and photos tacked to the face, a couple of posters strewn about the walls: one of a banana-yellow Porsche 911 and one for *The Walking Dead*. Some other posters have been balled into unrecognizable chunks of paper on the floor.

His desk is a disaster; notebooks, papers, and books strewn about, haphazardly covering the surface. One huge computer monitor in the center, the screen black. There is, however, a really nice recording set up free standing next to the desk, a video camera on a tripod, a round, white, professional quality recording mic below it. There's even a silver dome, dormant bulb inside, all ready to light up the show. I'm about to ask about it, wondering if he's a secret YouTuber or something, when something else catches my attention. Near the corner of his wall, there's a huge chunk of broken plaster, as if someone put their fist through it.

I point to it jokingly. "I hope that wall owed you money."

"Shouldn't you be on a date with Reid or something?" His voice is firm, sharp, and cracks like a whip against me.

"Ouch," I say, "Did Cole tell you he was spying on me? Or did you put him up to it?"

He folds his arms across his chest, his expression sour, his mouth clamped shut, a muscle in the back of his jaw twitching.

"Well, first of all, it wasn't a date. We're friends. Friends hang out." I narrow my eyes, "But secondly, and most importantly, I don't owe you an explanation or an apology. And I certainly don't appreciate your friends spreading useless gossip."

He shakes his head, turning away. "If you're here to back out of homecoming, just say so."

I hold up my hands. "Slow down, turbo. Who said anything about backing out? I want to go to the dance with you. I only came by because I was worried. You were out of school last week, and now this..."

"I'm fine."

I decide to probe, realizing it may be my only

chance. "Are you taking anything for it? Antibiotics or anything?"

He rolls his eyes. "No, Farris. I'm not diseased or anything. I've just got a headache."

"Okay," I say, trying to meet his eyes. "Is there anything I can do? You need anything?"

He closes his eyes. "I'm just tired. You should go."

I shake my head. I'm still angry, but I don't want to leave things like this. "You realize you're kinda being a dick, right? And even so, I'm still here, wanting to help." I take a breath. "Look, I know how miserable being sick can make you, so I'm giving you one pass. *One*. But if I walk out this door right now, feeling like this, I can't guarantee I'll ever walk in it again."

It's an ultimatum, I know. And as much as I hate giving them, I've been scorned enough to know I won't ever let myself feel that way again. I won't be with someone who puts that on me. Life's too short.

When he doesn't answer, I back away, rubbing my hands down my jeans. "Okay, well, see you around then."

I move toward his doorway.

His eyes pop open, and he leaps off the rumpled bed. His arm comes across my face, preventing me from crossing the threshold. I feel myself tense at his closeness, and not in a good way.

"Hey, listen. I don't mean to be a jerk. I'm just crazy exhausted, and when Cole mentioned seeing you and Reid, I dunno, it just got under my skin. Please don't be angry. I'm really glad you came by."

I turn to face him. His eyes are inches from mine. "Of course," I whisper hoarsely.

He moves forward, slowly, hesitantly, closing the distance between our lips. The kiss is sweet and timid. He whispers an apology against my mouth, and I nod.

This time, when he pulls back, I grab him, bringing him back to me, kissing him roughly, hungrily, until the last fragments of anger have fallen off me. When I pull back, he smiles, and I wipe my ChapStick residue off his bottom lip with my thumb.

"See you tomorrow," I say, slipping out and closing the door behind me with a soft click.

WHEN I ARRIVE HOME, DAD HAS HIS NOSE GLUED TO A football game he's recorded. The Cowboys must be losing, because the long string of expletives emanating from the living room, all ending with "Romo," would have made a sailor blush.

"Hey, kiddo, you girls have a good time tonight?" he asks as I lay the dress bag over the back of the chair.

"Yep. Got a cute dress and some accessories," I say, digging his credit card out of my wallet and handing it back to him.

He jerks his head over his shoulder. "Put it by my wallet on the kitchen counter," he says, and then is immediately distracted by the sound of a referee blowing a whistle on screen. "You're damn right that was offensive interference!" He pauses, and I gather my dress. Before I can make a clean getaway, he calls out over his shoulder, "What was the damage?"

I grimace, telling him the final total. He whistles.

"I hope you plan on getting married in that dress," he jokes, turning his full attention back to the TV.

"So eager to get rid of me?" I say, slinging the dress over my shoulder.

"Well, you do eat a lot," he says absently. "On the other hand, without you around, who would do the dishes and take out the trash?"

I give him a mock salute and head for the kitchen. There, on the counter, is Dad's wallet, keys, and cell phone. I drop the card atop the black leather wallet and lift the phone, pocketing it before I can change my mind.

I know I shouldn't do it, but I am already this far.

Making a beeline for my room, I spare a quick glance at the TV. It's only seven minutes into the third quarter. I have just enough time to do what I need to and get the phone back before he notices it missing. Unless it rings, of course. Quickly, I flip it to silent, dropping the gown on my bed and turning for the office.

After connecting the phone to my computer, it

takes me all of three minutes to get past his passcode and into the firmware on the phone. I pull up the email, still sitting in his inbox. Opening it, I back trace to the point of origin. Whoever sent it is really good, not a rank amateur sending something from his mom's computer. The message routes through three server farms, before coming to a dead end at a bulletproof host in China. I tuck my hair behind my ears with both hands, and then crack my knuckles before trying something else.

Finally, I have what little info I can find scrawled on a hot pink Post-it note. The date the email was sent, the time it was sent, and a tiny scrap of data stored layered in the original message, one word, repeating over and over.

Splice.

It's not much—not nearly enough—but it's all I'm going to get. I sit back, unplugging the phone and pondering my options.

Sneaking to the kitchen for a cup of coffee, I replace the phone, grab my drink, and return to my desk. I decide to try from the other end.

Bianca is the strongest possibility, and right now, the only real suspect. I already know she has the know-how to pull it off. But she herself admitted that her mother was initially blamed for the screw-ups. So what's her motive? Does she have mommy issues and want to get her in trouble? Was it unintentional? Until I have some kind of motive, I don't dare mention it to anyone.

But that doesn't mean I can't track her online. Opening up the Omega Portal, I search through until I find the black market, the buy and sell corner of the dark web. Most people only see about ten percent of the Internet in their lives, the white-washed, government approved areas. But the Internet is so much bigger and more dangerous than that. Omega Portal is the seedy underbelly, haven to hackers, designers, and perverts alike. It's a no-holds-barred, anything-goes area that would scare the average Joe so badly they might never sleep again. I scan through the most recent listings and chat areas. Scrolling past someone selling software that will let you remote access a cell phone's mic and camera, I find the thread I'm looking for. A conversation from last week—one of the usernames is oSplice.

I grab the profile and trace the activity back. oSplice has been very busy, and it takes me the better part of three hours to find what I'm looking for. The screen goes red, a single image stark in the center of my monitor. It's a black Rottweiler with three heads, each baring fangs. The dog is Cerberus, the guardian of the Underworld in classic Greek mythology. Under each head is a white rectangle with a blinking curser, a password port.

I sit back in my chair, my hands falling from the keyboard. Either the site requires three separate passwords to access, or you only get three attempts to enter the correct one, and I have no idea which. All I know is that my standard algorithm won't work on it. Hacking a password is essentially like picking a lock; you go through, trying each possibility until the tumblers fall into place. But this... this is far too sophisticated for that. The only way in would be to get myself into oSplice's computer and find the passwords stored there.

The dog growls and the screen blinks three times, dumping me back in the main chat area of the Omega Portal.

Oh, and apparently, I have a time limit too.

Delightful.

Then, I decide to try something a little more basic. Retrieving the list of names from my backpack, I type in the first one and hit the search button. To my surprise, something hits. I click the link and am taken to a video of what looks like a child's birthday party, uploaded six years ago. I try the next and the next, catching everything from photos clearly hijacked from their phones to text message archives. Finally, I type in the name I've been avoiding. Oliver's name.

A string of videos pop up, the most recent dated three weeks prior. I click it, and he's sitting in his room, strumming a guitar, singing an old Beetles song. I watch, hypnotized by him, by the way his fingers pluck each chord, the way his voice sounds, so sad and melodic, but mostly, by the way the light catches his eyes when he occasionally looks up into the camera. Closing it out, I scroll through the others. They are all set to private—not that that really means anything on the Internet—but I can't help wondering why he's hiding such a talent. Between his looks and his voice, he could be an overnight Internet sensation; I've seen huge careers begin with less. Each video is basically the same, just him, singing. I close the last one, feeling like I've just breeched a chasm between us, or possibly, horribly overstepped my bounds, invaded his privacy.

Feeling guilt twist in my gut, I shove the list back into my backpack, knocking it off the desk and scattering its contents onto the floor. Another folded paper falls out, and I clutch it in my hand. Without even opening it, I know it is Oliver's note. I read and reread it so many times, the edges are worn and the ink smeared.

Rocking back in my chair, I remember the mysterious white pills. Getting back on the computer, I do a search for the numbers, but nothing comes up. That alone makes the small hairs rise to attention on the back of my neck. Retrieving the image from my phone, I try searching the online pharmacy guide, but again, nothing hits. Then, I decide to use the power of the Omega Portal in my favor. Posting the link in a chat window under my nic, Cypher464, I caption it, *'Found these. Anyone know if they are a good high?'* Then, while I'm waiting, I scroll through images of steroids and opiates and known club drugs. Nothing matches the pills, and no one responds to my posting.

There's obviously only one way I'm ever going to figure out the truth, I'm just going to have to break down and ask Oliver about it. No matter how cute or charming he is, if he's using drugs, it's a deal breaker. Deep down, I wonder if that's what's keeping me from just saying something.

When I turn everything off and head back to my room, the blinking lights of my alarm clock read 2:16 am. I change quickly and slip into bed, expecting my brain to be too engaged to sleep, but exhaustion wins and soon I'm out cold.

ELEVEN

MY SLEEP IS RESTLESS, FULL OF DREAMS OF DRUGS and winding up at homecoming naked and dateless. Then it grows darker. The dreams become me, under water as the tide rolls over me, tossing me to and fro under the surface. I reach upward, kicking my legs, but I'm pinned below. I just can't force myself up through the surf. My lungs burn as I fight to hold the last, precious breath inside and my legs cramp with each desperate flail, but I can't surface. There's no escape. Some distant part of my brain tells me to relax, to let myself sink, but I can't. I writhe and I fight even as each new wave rolls overhead. Through the chaos, I hear my mom's voice, singing lullabies in the darkness.

Startled, I bolt out of bed, falling onto the hard floor with a grunt. My clock read 5:45. I run my hands through my hair and try to push the images out of my mind.

Maybe I should ask Dad about going back to therapy.

The alarm wails, the sound echoing through my small room. I get to my feet, untangling my blankets from my legs, and slap it off, reluctantly heading for the shower.

On the way to school, I fill Reid in on my final plan for getting into the guidance counselor's office. As it turns out, I'll need more help than I had originally thought, which means trusting Derek and Kayla with at least the basics of what I was up to. I swear them to secrecy, and then start talking. By the time I'm done, they both look at me as if seeing me for the first time, a weird mixture of surprise and excitement.

Kayla agrees eagerly and Derek shrugs, content to follow wherever she leads. I notice as he looks out the window, a large, red welt is visible under the neckline of his black Henley. I want to ask him about it, but Kayla catches me looking at it and pointedly shakes her head, silencing me. In the back of my mind, another plan forms. One that has nothing at all to do with the squadron or the person hacking it. I push it to the back of my thoughts, letting it unspool in the background while I draw my focus forward to other things.

When I lay out my plan in detail, Derek nods.

"You have a truly devious mind," Reid says.

"Finally, four years of drama class is going to pay off," Kayla adds, a bit maniacally, as she rubs her hands together.

Oliver is back at school, apologizing again for his behavior the night before as he walks me to class. When I tell him I won't be at lunch that day, he frowns.

"I hope this isn't about how I acted," he begins. "I'll do anything to make it up to you, I swear."

"No, it's not that. I have a meeting with Mrs. Groves," I say lamely.

He recovers quickly. "Well, there's always tomorrow," he says, kissing the tip of my nose before leaving me to head to his own class.

We don't see each other much through the morning, and after third period, I hurry to the second floor.

There's a small waiting area, a few chairs, and a tall, round table scattered with brochures for various colleges strewn about. When she opens her door, greeting me with a friendly smile, I shudder. The last time I found myself sitting in a guidance office had been because someone had spray painted the word slut in bold, white letters across my locker, and somehow, it was my fault. I'd been told that maybe if I dressed nicer, smiled more, was more approachable, I'd have more friends. Never mind the fact that I'd committed the cardinal sin of narcing out a party, gotten half the lacrosse team suspended for underage drinking, and the most popular boy in school ended up on probation for possession. Naw, all I needed was a little lip gloss and a dress to make people like me again.

Steeling myself, I step into her office. A desk, a few chairs, piles of papers and books, file cabinets, lots of artwork—most of it homemade—and a computer so old there might have been pictures of it in the Great Pyramid of Giza. Though I don't look, I hear the secure server humming behind the slim closet door to my left.

"So, what can I do for you today?" the stubby woman asks, her kind, brown eyes wrinkling at the corners.

She has a puckered mouth and her gray hair hangs, black at the tips as if she had once colored it but had stopped years ago. She isn't fat exactly, but the kind of overweight that comes from spending all day sitting at a desk. Her pinstriped suit strains in the middle, though the white, gauzy blouse underneath looks five sizes too big, draping from her frame in odd places.

"Well, I had a few problems at my old school and I wondered if that stuff was going to hurt my chances of going Ivy League after graduation," I begin smoothly.

Okay, it isn't entirely a lie, but the best lies are based partially in truth. Honestly, the top five hundred honor students in the country would have to die for me to have even a snowball's chance in hell at Ivy League. I know this. She knows this. But she can't just come out and crush my dreams, she will need to gently steer me in another direction.

Her ancient computer winds to life as she types in my name. She leans forward, reading my file, and frowns. What she's seeing is probably the fact that at my last school, I'd been kicked off the newspaper for reporting that my principal had been altering grades for athletes to keep their basketball team in the state finals. The allegations were completely true, but I'd gotten canned anyway. Or the time I'd gotten suspended for a week for fighting. Never mind that I'd been jumped in the girls' bathroom and was only defending myself. Or, possibly, that one time, I'd refused to sit in class and listen to my computer applications teacher try to teach me how to use an Excel spreadsheet. I'd told him I'd come back when he could teach me something I didn't already know, gotten up, and walked out. At first, he'd threatened to fail me, then, after he handed me the end-of-the-year exam and I passed it with flying colors, he let me just sit in his office during class and design website templates, which he then sold and split the profits with me.

Absently wondering which story is putting that magically delicious frown on her face, I slide my hand into my backpack, feeling around for my phone. I find it and hit the send button.

There's a loud series of thuds, then wailing and shouting in the hallway.

"What's that?" I ask loudly.

Mrs. Groves stands quickly, tells me to wait where I am, and then leaves the office, closing the door behind her. I don't know what Kayla did to cause the commotion, but whatever it is, it worked. By now, Derek has taken up his position outside the door and is acting as lookout. He gives me a quick thumbs-up through the glass panel beside the door.

Slipping into the empty desk chair, I plug my flash drive into her machine, minimize my file, and start pulling up the confidential files for each student on my list, dropping them onto the drive. I still have Oliver's file at home, but I haven't looked at it yet so I decide to throw it on the drive anyway, just in case there's something on here that never made it to the hard copy, which can sometimes happen. Guilt stabs at me again. It's like all I've done all week is invade his privacy. If he'd done something like that to me, I'd have kicked him to the curb. Yet here I am, being a filthy hypocrite. Again.

I'll only look at his last, if I haven't found anything on someone else, I promise myself.

Derek coughs and steps forward, out of my line of sight. I hear him exchanging words with Mrs. Graves.

"You'll just have to make an appointment some time later. I'm with someone right now," she says curtly.

Derek tries to protest, but she says something else and dismisses him.

I'm back in my chair, flash drive tucked into my front pocket, when she strides through the open door. "Is everything all right?" I ask.

"Yes, Kayla Pierce took a fall down the stairs, but it looks like she's alright," she says coolly.

"Oh, Kayla's a friend of mine, Mrs. Groves. Do you mind if we do this later? I'd like to go check on her." I try to infuse concern, rather than amusement, into my voice.

She pauses. "Oh, of course. She's in the nurse's office."

I thank her, gather my stuff, and bolt from the room before I can burst out laughing. I'd asked for a distraction, and Kayla threw herself down the stairs, going full-tilt drama queen.

Of course she did.

Reid meets up with me outside the library. "You get what you need?"

I hold up the drive. "I sure hope so." I pause, tapping it on my chin. "What I don't understand is why? Why would anyone here want to threaten a squadron? I mean, it's bad news for all of us, right?"

Now it's his turn to shrug. "It could be an attention thing. Or a rage thing. Or even a boredom thing. Why do people do anything?"

I tilt my head. "That's the thing. People are generally predictable. You act because you need something or want something. So what does threatening a squadron get you?" I hold up a hand, counting on my fingers. "Typical motives are revenge, love, money, ego, and power."

"Not ego, probably, or they would have signed their name," Reid reasons. "Probably not money. You can't exactly sell grounding a squadron."

I pause, something clicking into place in my brain as Bianca's words flitter through my mind. "You can buy and sell anything. Actually, if you created a program that could screw with military aircraft on-board computers, that'd be worth a fucking fortune to the right buyers."

"Ok, so money is a maybe. But my money is still on love. The squadron gets locked down, no deployment. No leaving your family behind."

"But you can't sustain it. Say the squadron gets grounded, permanently, what do they do? They just send everyone out to other squadrons. It's a temporary reprieve at best."

"It's a helluva risk to take anyway," Reid adds. "I'm sure the DOJ is all over this. And probably Homeland too. Eventually, they will find the person responsible."

"And when they do, that person will be put in a very dark hole for a very long time." I shake my head. "I just don't get it."

TWELVE

E VEN WITH ALL THE INFO I NABBED FROM THE counselor, I still only have one real suspect. My pick for crazy bitch is Bianca Peterson. According to her file, she has a history of behavior problems and has attempted suicide twice. Her parents thought she was acting out, desperate for attention. All signs point to her, like neon lights. So why is there something, nagging, in the pit of my stomach that's not convinced?

Proof. I need solid proof. And the sooner the better. If she is behind it, I can take the info to my dad. He'll be pissed I ignored his order to leave it alone, but I'll happily take that over something really bad happening. If this is about money, if she really is looking for someone to buy the code she created to screw with the planes, come hell or high water, I'll stop her.

But, after jumping the gun one too many times before, I've also learned the value of patience, of knowing all the facts before ruining someone's life, especially when that life might be your own.

Sitting at my desk, I stare at Oliver's record. I'd managed not to open the digital file, but something about having the hard copy right here in front of me is like having an itch I can't quite scratch. Finally, I give in.

I need to be thorough, after all. I need to be positive.

Sure enough, everything Reid told me is true. Oliver has been suspended six times in three years, all for fighting. There's one note in particular that really bothers me, a note from the school counselor saying that Oliver has violent and depressed moods and that he might be dangerous to himself and others. Then, something must have changed over last spring break, because the notes end abruptly, replaced by reports from his teachers saying how well he's doing in class. Taking a glance at his grades, I see he's gone from Ds and Fs, to straight As in the last two years. A jaded, cynical part of me wonders if he's done it himself, or if being the star quarterback has more to do with it.

I close the folder. Maybe he had been taking drugs freshman year. If he managed to get himself clean, that would explain the miraculous change in personality. I tuck the file away, intending to have Reid return it to the school tomorrow. My computer dings, a reminder I've all but forgotten I set.

Clicking it on, I navigate back to the Omega

Portal video stream where Oliver uploads his music. A new upload came in today, a slow, haunting rendition of *The End of The World As We Know It* by REM. The image flickers, and I frown. Pulling the file, I open the properties and find something else, a hidden stream of video behind the first. Carefully extracting it, I open it in a separate window.

It's just flashes, images and clips of video, no sound, but somehow, that only makes it more disturbing. It's spliced images of people cutting themselves, women crying, flies on a child's body, an eerie white mask, dead trees—so much flying across the screen I can't catch half of it. But the end, the clip that drives the shiver of dread up my spine, is a single hand, reaching out from below the surface of dark, swirling water. Then, as suddenly as it began, the video vanishes. It is once more just Oliver, playing his guitar. When I try to access the embedded footage again, it's gone. Vanished.

A glitch? Someone piggybacking the file for some other purpose? Or a onetime view and kill? I rub my cold fingertips across my lips once before closing the site.

I spend the better part of the next couple of days following Bianca around the school. I ask her about her project, even offering to help, but she rebuffs me.

"No thanks. I think I have what I need."

During class, I sneak out, pick her lock and

search her locker, hoping to find her laptop inside. My search turns up nothing but candy wrappers, books, and a picture of her with Cassy and some guy, his face burnt out. This girl clearly has issues, if nothing else. Delving into full research mode on her, I learn that her mother is an admin clerk in the parts department, and that her dad is a manager at the commissary. According to her social media, she came out as gay only six months ago, and the response has been mostly positive. There were, of course, a handful of guys offering to "change her mind" and one aunt who alternately told her she would pray for her, and then disowned her.

Unfortunately, she keeps her laptop close at hand, generally stuffed in her oversized designer purse. There's not a single window I can crawl through to get a peek. I spend the bulk of Wednesday night creating a data worm. If I can just plug it into her computer, it will find the information I need in a matter of minutes. The trick will be getting close enough to use it.

As I sneak to bed late Wednesday night, I overhear Dad on the phone in his room. Stopping to listen, I take a single step toward his door, which is ajar.

"Yeah, the Feds have hit a dead end, which just makes it worse. I've interviewed every single soldier in my squadron; I doubt any of them have the desire—much less the know-how, to pull this off. Yes. Yes.

The biggest concern right now is the security of the fleet. Yes, sir. Yes. I'll keep you informed." He hesitates, "We're exploring that option as well. But the results are positive. We should be able to resume flights Monday."

My breath catches in my throat. The two-week down period has ended quicker than expected. This is bad. This is so bad. I hear him sign off and I tap gently on his door.

"Yep?"

I open the door. He meets my eyes, sighing from where he sits on the edge of his bed. "I assume you were eavesdropping?"

I nod. "Hard not to."

He waves me in, and I stand in front of him. "If you've got something to say, then out with it. I'm bushed and I need to hit the rack," he demands, his voice tense and tired.

I press my lips together, exhaling through my nose before speaking. "I don't think it's a good idea to start the flights again." I say in a rush. He opens his mouth, but I hold up my hand. "It's just... you still don't know who did this, or why. If their intent was to ground the planes, or to get someone's attention, or even to prove they've found a way to hack the onboard systems, then by flying again, you force them to escalate. This time, someone could get hurt, or worse." I let my voice drop on the last word.

He holds a hand out, and I take it. "I appreciate

your concern, and you're right. But the Feds think they are close to tracking the hack, and in the meantime, we're in the process of shielding all the electronics. You don't need to worry. I've got everything under control."

I frown, but his face is stern and etched with deep lines. He's on edge, but trying to play calm for me. I can say more, but again, without proof, I've got nothing, so I shut my mouth and nod once.

For now, at least, I'm going to have to let him deal with it. And pray to God that I'm wrong.

BY THE TIME FRIDAY NIGHT ROLLS AROUND, I'M totally on edge. I haven't seen Dad in days. He's working pretty much round the clock to get the new components installed, tested, and approved for flight before Monday, sort of an all-hands-on-deck situation he assures me in a hastily left voicemail telling me, again, not to worry.

As if that is possible.

Derek, Kayla, and Reid opt to skip the game, no big surprise, so I decide to go with Georgia. She's the only one of her friends not on the pom-pom brigade, and she seems glad to have some company in the stands. I wonder, for a few minutes, if she'd notice me sneaking off to the locker room to get my hands on Bianca's laptop. The only thing that keeps me from going for it is the probability that she left it at home for the game.

Finally, with Georgia's encouragement, I relax and allow myself to enjoy the game. We cheer and wave our newly purchased foam fingers as our brave team is stomped into the dirt by Havelock High School. After the final horn blows, signaling the end of the game, we rush down the bleachers and wait for the guys in the tunnel that leads to the locker room.

I wait, wringing my hands, unsure if Oliver will be glad to see me after the loss. But when he pulls off his helmet and finds me waiting, his face lights up with delight, his dimple making a star appearance. He walks toward me, covered in sweat and mud, and I realize he's never looked as good to me as he does right now. His smile warm, face flushed, short hair glistening with sweat.

"You came." He smiles.

"I told you I would." Stepping forward, I throw my arms around his neck carelessly and plant a kiss on his warm mouth.

He squeezes me gently, lifting me off my feet. "If that's what I get when I lose, I can't wait to see what happens when I win." He laughs, pulling back.

"I was just on my way home, but I wanted to say hi before I left," I say, leaning back against the concrete wall.

"I'm glad you did. I'll pick you up tomorrow night at seven?" he confirms.

"I'll be ready."

"I heard you got a dress. Guess that means I'll have to look halfway decent, too," he jokes, tucking his helmet under his arm.

"Don't get too fancy. I fully plan on wearing sneakers. You ever notice no matter how slow zombies shuffle, they always catch you? I'm not taking any chances."

"Sneakers it is, then."

He kisses my cheek and jogs down the hallway, smacking Trey on the back of the head as he passes. Trey, who'd been about to kiss Georgia, backs off and follows, shouting profanities as they run.

Georgia leans over, her arms folded across her chest. "You know, I haven't seen Ollie this happy in a really long time."

I'm not sure what to say to that and when I don't respond, she faces me directly.

"Just, be careful with him, okay? He's more fragile than he looks," she adds.

GEORGIA SHOWS UP AT MY DOOR ON SATURDAY afternoon, with a crate of makeup, a bag of hair tools, and a six-pack of Mountain Dew.

"I could totally kiss you right now," I say, letting her in.

She smirks. "I know."

We smear some cold, blue mud on our faces and

she paints my nails while they dry.

"So, how long have you been with Trey?" I ask as she sits me back to pluck my eyebrows.

"Oh, about two years now. It was one of those things. We'd been friends forever, and then... suddenly, it was more, you know."

I murmur yes, but truthfully, I've never been in that situation. My first and only boyfriend had been sort of a whirlwind thing. We'd met at school and three days later, we were making out in the back of his pickup. He was cute, and I was too young and stupid to realize he had a reputation for seducing freshmen.

"What about you? What was it like at your last school?" she asks, and I feel myself tense, just as she rips another stray hair from my face.

"Ever read the Inferno?" I ask.

She makes a face. "Can't say that I have."

"Well, let's just say that I'm pretty sure there is an eleventh circle of hell, and that's it."

She chuckles. "That bad, huh?"

"You have no idea," I mutter, trying to keep my mouth as still as possible so the now-dry mask doesn't crack.

She washes my hair in the sink, and then blow-dries it straight. We wash off the masks, slather on some lotion, and she begins applying my makeup. Truth is, I'm glad to have the help and the company. Georgia is the perfect balance of friendly without being annoying. While she works, she chats about idle things, TV shows she loves, a summer trip she took with her family to Hawaii. It's just enough to keep my mind off everything else.

By the time she finishes, my hair hangs in perfect curls framing my face, which despite the amount of makeup she put on, manages to look feminine and soft. She's done something that makes my eyes stand out and painted my lips a deep red that complements the jeweled vines of my dress. I feel pretty. Girlie.

Not that I'd ever wear something this high-maintenance on a regular basis. I will have to keep a tube of lipstick in my microscopic bag for touch-ups, and I'm forbidden from rubbing my eyes—no matter how much they itch—or from running my fingers through my hair, lest I pull out all the hard-fought curls.

As good as his word, Oliver arrives at the stroke of seven, bearing a delicate red rose corsage in a funny-looking plastic container. He blushes as he slips it onto my wrist. I wish my mom could be here for this. A deep, familiar ache blossoms in my chest and my eyes dart to her photograph on the bookshelf. She would smile and take pictures while Dad stood in the corner looking terrifying. Then she would hug me and tell me how beautiful I look.

But the house is empty, except for Oliver and me. There's no one to take a photo, no one to remind him I'm to be home by midnight and no later. Just silence and the sound of my heart beating in my ears. Taking my hand, Oliver draws me close.

"You look amazing," he says softly. "I'm kinda glad no one else is here, so I can do this."

With that, he steps forward, putting his hands on my waist and pulling me into a deep, long kiss. When he pulls back, it's like he's taking all the air with him, and for a moment, I forget how to breathe. I open my eyes, expecting to see his face smeared red and looking like a clown from my lipstick, but there's not a single smudge. Score one for Georgia's fabulous makeup crate.

"I can't get over how beautiful you look," Oliver says, leading me out to his truck and opening the door for me.

"You don't look half bad yourself," I say appreciatively.

Actually, he's incredibly debonair in his classic black suit with his long, red tie and vest. Georgia must have helped him pick it out because it goes perfectly with my dress. He has kept his promise, however, and his shoes are dark blue Nike runners. Helping me into the cab, he notices my red Chuck Taylors and smirks.

The dance is being held in the Grand Ballroom at the Officers' Club.

The theme is masquerade and there are masks, balloons, and streamers, all reflecting the thousands of tiny twinkle lights strung from the ceiling. The tables are covered in black-and-gold silk, and each one has a tall, silver candelabrum erupting from the center.

As soon as we arrive, a boy in a black top hat and tails snaps our picture. I spot Derek and Kayla sitting at a table with Georgia and Trey, chatting away. Trey is saying something I can't make out, and Derek is actually smiling.

Derek is wearing an old-fashioned burgundy velvet tux with long tails, the ruffles of his white shirt spilling out over the neckline and at the wrists. It's very Gothic. Very Derek. Kayla sits beside him in her green-and-black tutu, her hair hanging in loose burgundy-and-green waves. Green ballet slippers with ribbons that wrap around her legs up to her knees. Georgia is her polar opposite in a floor-length pastel-pink silk gown that hugs her chest before crisscrossing down to her waist. Her blonde hair is pinned at the top of her head, hundreds of delicate ringlets cascading from a small tiara. Both girls spot me at the same time and wave.

"I invited Derek and Kayla to sit with us. Hope you don't mind," Oliver whispers, leaning in and placing a gentle kiss on my ear.

It's his gift, I realize. His peace offering. His apology. His way of telling me that he not only respects my choices, but that he wouldn't try to pull me to one side or the other. He wants me to be happy, whatever that might mean. I squeeze his hand tightly, mouthing thanks before turning back to the table and waving. Without warning, a familiar tune bursts through the speakers, bringing everyone to their feet. Oliver spins me onto the dance floor and we move, a rhythmic mass of bodies around us, but my focus is all on him, on the way we move together, apart and back together again, perfectly in sync. A slow song starts and before I can catch my breath, he's holding me tightly against him, his hand in mine, swaying to the music.

For a brief minute, it is as if the rest of the world falls away, leaving us alone in the universe. The feel of his hand on the small of my back, the smell of him—it is better than anything my feeble imagination could have conjured. Laying my head against his shoulder, I let everything else go—lead balloons I've been holding on too for far too long. My guilt, my worry, my fear, it all floats away and the only thing still holding me together is Oliver.

In that moment, I resolve to tell him everything. About my past, about my mom, about the things going on with my dad and how I am looking into it, even about reading his file and snooping in his bathroom. I've been holding him at arm's length for long enough.

Maybe it's time to let him in.

Leaning back, I open my mouth to speak, but the words are swallowed by the music as the slow song ends, fading seamlessly into a faster, pounding rhythm. Around us, people swarm the floor in groups, jumping and dancing and laughing as the lights pulse in time with the beat. After a few more songs, I'm panting and sweating. We take a seat at our table, and Derek brings over an armful of waters as Georgia and Trey are announced homecoming king and queen to a chorus of cheers and whistles. I watch them, parting the crowd like Moses parting the Red Sea, making their way onstage. We clap loudly. Oliver shouts, "Go Trey!" as they're crowned. Another slow song begins, and Oliver looks at me. I hold up a hand.

"Gonna have to sit this one out." I pat my chest.

I drain my water cup quickly. Oliver stands, offering, over the loud music, to go for punch. He crosses the dance floor to the refreshment table, but instead of coming right back, he cuts through the swathe of people and slips out the back doors.

It's the strangest sensation, like the world is crashing down around me, slivers of noise and movement being pulled away in slow motion. Suddenly, I'm standing outside of everything, things are moving around me, but it feels distant, surreal.

I try to talk myself out of it, even as I follow him. My mind spins, listing off a million things he could be doing, all totally innocent. But there's something else, a relentless thirst for the truth, and a cold certainty that whatever is going on, he's been keeping something from me. I can't trust him; I can't open myself up to him, however much I might want to.

The bottom line is, deep down, I don't want to be right.

And if it is drugs, and I break things off, there's the very real possibility I'll see a repeat of what happened at my last school. I could very easily find myself a social outcast. Hopefully this time, I'd at least still have Derek and Kayla. And Reid. Guilt washes over me as I realize that it's the first time I've thought of him all weekend. It's the kind of guilt you get when you leave for school and realize you forgot to feed your dog, the guilt you feel because something or someone wasn't important enough for you to remember. He's been a good friend and he deserves better from me, and whatever happens, I swear to myself that I'll make it up to him.

When I find Oliver, he's standing out in the corridor, a pill bottle in his hand, taking a drink from my plastic cup.

"What's going on?" I ask, trying to keep the accusation out of my voice.

He slips the bottle into his pocket as he turns to me. "Nothing. Why don't we go back inside?"

I take a deep breath, fortifying my resolve. It's now or never. "What are those pills?" I demand, folding my arms across my torso, hugging myself.

He stares at me for a moment before answering.

"What pills?"

I glare at him, getting angry now. He isn't going to make this easy, is he?

"I'm not stupid, Ollie. I saw the bottle, and I saw you taking them at your house the other day. I need to know," I say.

Taking a step back, his entire posture changes. He pulls himself up tall, his expression affronted. "You were spying on me?"

"No. I was walking by and I saw... It doesn't matter. The thing is, I won't be with someone who uses drugs. So if that's what's going on, just tell me now."

"I don't have to explain anything to you," he practically growls.

I shake my head. "No, you don't. But I wish you would. Maybe I can help you, or help you find someone who can." It sounds feeble, even to me.

He laughs and it's dry, sarcastic.

"What's funny?" I demand, folding my arms across my chest.

"You can't fix this, Farris. There's no magic wand you can wave to fix me like a broken piece of pottery." He opens his mouth to say something else, then closes it as a noisy group of kids pour out of the ballroom, laughing and talking. They move down the hallway toward the bathrooms, staring back at us.

He takes me by the elbow, opening the metal

door marked Exit, and pulls me outside.

The grass is wet under my shoes, making it slippery as he leads me across the lawn to a gazebo on the edge of a small pond. The only light comes from the distant glow of the party raging inside. He drops my arm, leaning over the railing.

"Why do you assume it's drugs?" he asks thoughtfully, his temper waning in the cool night air.

I consider lying, but what point is there in it now? "Reid said something about it. He said he caught you using and that's why you aren't friends anymore," I say slowly.

Without looking at me, he pounded his fists against the wood. "I just bet he did," he says bitterly.

"Why don't you tell me your side of the story?" I suggest, smoothing the back of my dress carefully and sitting on the step.

He sighs. "There are some things I wish I could tell you about Reid, but I can't. I swore I wouldn't tell anyone, and I won't break that promise. But I will say that I don't do drugs." He pauses. "Not the illegal kind, anyway."

I wait for him to say more, but he doesn't. The silence hangs between us for a few heartbeats.

"I jump to conclusions; I'm a conclusion jumper. And I ask for honesty, even when I can't give it myself. I'm a hypocrite, and sometimes, even a liar. I keep people I care about at a distance because I'm so scared to trust anyone that it makes me physically sick." I hold up my hands. "I wanted to trust you. Something inside kept telling me I should. But part of me knew you were hiding things. I don't know. We all have our secrets, me as much as anyone. Maybe I have no right to ask you to trust me with yours."

I stand, dusting off my butt.

"It's lithium," he whispers into the darkness, "for my bipolar disorder."

I turn to him, my eyebrows drawing together over my nose. Okay, not what I was expecting. Bipolar disorder. Everything suddenly clicks into place. The pills, the absences from school, the history of violent behavior that stopped so suddenly. Oliver isn't psychotic; he's just doing his best to manage an illness that isn't his fault. Glancing up, I see fear in his eyes. Fear that I'm going to... what? Reject him? Mock him? Decide it's all too much and walk away? Surely, he knows me better than that.

I laugh. Not at his fear or his pain, but at the fact that he thought something like that would matter to me at all.

"You think it's funny?" he snaps.

"Sorry. No. It's just that I was wondering if you'll ever stop surprising me." I walk over to him, covering his heart with one hand. "From the moment I met you, I knew there was something different about you. Something in how you spoke and how you moved and in how you never did quite what I expected you to. I thought I was going nuts. It's like I have this internal compass that points me where I want to go. Then suddenly, there you were, and everything was spinning. It all makes sense now."

Oliver lays a hand on the side of my face. "You mean, you aren't weirded out? You don't think I'm a freak?" Hesitantly, he reaches up and cups the side of my neck in his other hand. "You don't hate me?"

I smile, leaning my face into his palm. "Of course not. I'm glad you finally told me the truth," I say. His eyes light up like a kid on Christmas morning, like he's just gotten everything he ever wished for. I feel very unworthy of that look. "But, I meant what I said. There are things about me you don't know. I will tell you, I swear I will. I just need, maybe a little time."

I shake my head. "I told you, I'm a terrible hypocrite."

He leans forward, resting his forehead on mine. "I don't want to lose you, Farris. No one has ever made me feel the way you do, like I could be a normal guy with a normal life. Like I could be in love." He freezes as the words escape his mouth, as if he's as surprised by them as I am. "I can't lose you."

I can think of only one way to reassure him of my feelings, and the second our lips meet, I know I feel the same. Any doubts about him are washed away in a rush of emotion. He crushes me against him, making my head swim. By the time we break apart, I'm flushed all over, aching with wanting to be closer, my heart beating frantically in my chest. I lean against him, letting him hold me as long as he's willing. Somehow, everything looks right from inside his arms.

"I'm sorry I didn't trust you," I say. "I should have. Some part of me always did. I've had so much on my mind lately, everything feels so unclear." I lean my head up, kissing his chin. "Everything but this."

He sighs, holding me a little tighter. "It's okay. I understand. I should have told you before."

I shake my head. "It's not okay. But I'll make it up to you."

He cocks his head to the side. "Really? Because I have some ideas..."

I can't help but grin at his suggestive tone. "Me, too."

A slow smile spreads across his face, and before I can say another word, he's kissing me again.

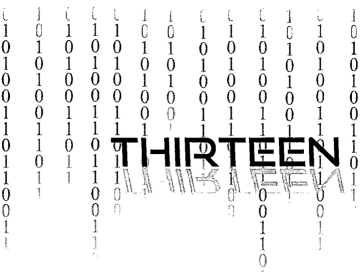

THIRTEEN

THE SUN PEEKING THROUGH MY CRAPPY BLINDS wakes me the next morning. My beautiful dress lays in a crumpled heap on my floor. I'd been so exhausted when I got home, I barely had the energy to pull it off before climbing into bed. Thinking back on the night, and on the intense make-out session at the pavilion, I smile, chewing the corner of my blanket as I squeal a little.

Getting up, I carefully hang the dress in my closet, running my hand over the fabric just once before slipping it into the plastic garment bag and moving it to its place on the black side. My therapist once suggested that my need to organize my clothing by color helped me bring order to chaos. I told him living with a Marine could make anyone neurotic.

My face is flushed when I make my way to the kitchen for coffee; I can feel it just like I can feel the wide, happy grin on my face. I feel lighter, one less thing on my *shit to stress about* list.

Dad makes pancakes in a clever attempt to avoid

conversation. Not that I mind. I have no intention of having a heart-to-heart with my father about my new boyfriend. Besides, there isn't much to tell. Always a gentleman, Oliver had given me a short, chaste kiss when he dropped me off, right before curfew. Though I was sure Dad was awake, he at least had the decency to not be waiting for me at the door, so I'd just slipped in and went to my room. Even now, just thinking about last night is enough to get my heart racing.

He loves me. He'd as good as said so. I stuff another forkful of pancakes into my mouth. We are still eating when the sirens go off.

Our heads snap up simultaneously. Dad grabs his phone the instant it rings. I can't make out the other end of the conversation, but from the look on his face, I know it's serious. Moments later my cell, still set to vibrate from the dance, goes off, buzzing across the table like an angry wasp. I pick it up, sliding it to answer. It's Reid's voice on the other end.

"Looks like you called it," he says, sounding tired. "Someone has stepped up their game."

"I'll call you back," I say quickly and disconnect.

"Dad?" I begin as he hangs up his phone.

He holds up his hand to stop me before I can say anything else. "There's been an explosion. It doesn't look like anyone was hurt. It was confined to the paint room, and there wasn't anyone up there this weekend. I have to go down and talk to the MPs."

He heads for his room to change, and I follow. "Do you think it's the same person who sent the email?" I ask through his closed door.

"Kid, these things can happen in a place with so many hazardous materials. It's probably just an accident."

I lean my back against the door, rolling my eyes. "I doubt it," I mumble and head for my bedroom.

We finish dressing at almost the same time, him in his khaki and green dress alphas, and me in my vintage Guns N' Roses T-shirt and black jeans.

"I'm going with you," I say flatly.

"Not this time, kid."

"Dad—"

"No. No discussion. I'll call you as soon as I know anything."

He gives me a peck on the forehead and leaves. I grab my flash drive off my desk and stuff it and my wallet in my messenger bag. Snatching my keys off the dining room table, I head for the door, making a call on my way out.

"Hello?" he answers.

"Reid, I'm on my way over."

REID'S PARENTS ARE HOME WHEN I GET THERE. HIS dad opens the door, and my saliva glands go into overdrive. He politely lets me in and leads me to the bedroom where Reid sits at his computer, his glasses reflecting the picture on the screen. His hair is tousled and his eyes bloodshot.

"Reid, you okay?" I ask, sitting down on the floor at the foot of his bed and pulling my knees up to my chest.

"Yeah. Long night. How was homecoming?"

I bite my lip. "It was kind of great, actually," I admit.

He shakes his head. "I still can't believe you want to date that macho asswipe." His tone is acidic as he swivels in his chair and stares at me like I'm the world's biggest idiot. "You read the file I gave you, right? Farris, that guy's dangerous. He may seem harmless right now, but he's a total Jekyll and Hyde."

I shake my head. "I know he had his issues, but he's past all that now."

He lowers his chin, looking at me over the top of his glasses. "Are you willing to bet your life on it?"

"Look, I wish I could explain, but I can't. Needless to say, I believe him. I trust him."

Reid's expression morphs to one of absolute exhaustion as he takes off his glasses and rubs his face. "I just don't want to see you get hurt," he says.

I want to reach out and touch him, but something tells me it's not a good idea. Even knowing that Oliver is the guy I want to be with, I still feel a pull to Reid that I can't quite explain—a kinship. Maybe I'm wrong. Maybe we can't be friends.

"Thanks," I mumble.

He nods and turns back to the computer, killing the power.

"What have you heard?" he asks, swiveling back to me.

"About the explosion? Not much. My dad thinks it might just be an accident," I say, tossing him the flash drive.

"Seriously?" His voice is tight. "That's a helluva coincidence, isn't it?"

"Delusional," I agree.

"Completely. You still looking at Bianca for this?" he asks, tapping the drive on his knee.

I sigh heavily. "She's my only suspect, but there's one problem."

"What's the issue?"

"I drove by her house on the way here. Her dad said she stayed the night with Cassy last night. I called Cassy and she confirmed. They stayed in all night, ordered pizza, and watched movies. She's still there right now. Whatever happened, she couldn't have done it. Besides, she may have the computer skills to pull off the email thing, but she's pulling a solid D in chemistry. If it was a chemical accident, do you really think she could have pulled that off?"

"Maybe Cassy is helping her? I've been tutoring her in chemistry; she's capable of coming up with something crude," he offers. "Of course, there's still one more possibility..."

I stand up. "It wasn't Oliver, if that's what you're

thinking."

"He has straight As in chemistry, he has been missing school right and left—yet somehow hasn't gotten kicked off the football team—and he's taking drugs."

I hold up my hand to stop him. "I told you, that's not what you think. Now, will you please drop it?"

"What if he was lying to you to cover up the truth?"

I frown, feeling my muscles coil in my back and arms. "Lay off about it, Reid."

Then he stands up, his eyes level with mine, his hands balled into fists.

"What's it going to take for you to see he's a *bad* guy? He may come across all sweet and sensitive, but he's not. He's *crazy*. Is it going to take someone getting hurt before you'll admit he could be responsible?" he fumes.

I snatch the drive off the floor where it'd fallen and storm out of the room. By the time I make it to my car, I'm crying. Not sad tears, just tears of frustration. Trust me, I know the difference. Then I think about what he'd said.

He's crazy....

Does Reid know about the bipolar disorder? If he does, wouldn't he know what the pills are for? None of it makes sense, and I can't exactly *ask* him about it without *telling* him about it. If Reid doesn't already know, I'm not going to be the one to let him in on it. If Oliver wants him to know, he'll say something. I wipe my eyes on my sleeves.

Not sure where else to go, I head for the squadron, figuring maybe I'll have lunch with Dad. When I pull into the parking lot, the hazmat crew is just leaving.

I rap on his door. "Dad, you here?" Gently, I push it open to find the room empty. His desk is tidy today, only a still-steaming cup of coffee occupying the space.

I kick back on the chair opposite his desk and put my feet up on the corner of it. An unfamiliar voice surprises me.

"Miss Barnett?" the S1 says, sticking her head into the room.

I jump, my feet falling noisily to the floor. "Um, yeah," I say.

"Your father's in a meeting. He should be back in a half an hour or so."

"Oh. Thanks. I'll just wait for him here." It isn't a question. I'm in a crappy mood, and I'm taking it out on her.

She shrugs and leaves, closing the door behind her, only to return a few minutes later with another cup of coffee.

"Here, I thought you might like this," she offers, holding it out to me.

I do like it, and I feel like a heel, which is a sensation I'm quickly getting accustomed to. "Thanks." I take the cup from her carefully.

The mug is old, a souvenir from the Marine Corps Birthday Ball three years earlier, judging by the lettering on the side. It's red with a chip on the handle, and it contains the strongest coffee I've ever tasted.

Not bad, though. Only a few weeks in and she's already making my dad's favorite kind of dear-God-what-is-this-sludge coffee. Either she's very efficient or she has a crush on my father. It wouldn't surprise me, really. Dad's pretty good looking, for an old guy. He hasn't dated anyone since Mom died, or at least not that I know of. I probably wouldn't hold it against him if he decided to start, but looking at the woman in front of me, I squirm at the mental image. Then I remember something that makes me relax. He couldn't date her even if he wanted to. He's an officer. There are rules against it. It's the first time I'd ever been thankful for Marine Corps regulations.

She smiles and leaves again. Bored, I pull my laptop out of my bag. I scan the headlines, check my email, and finished my trig homework before my dad finally gets back.

"Hey, kid," he says, planting a kiss on the top of my head as he passes and takes a seat in his high-backed chair. "What brings you here?"

I tuck my computer away. "I was thinking maybe we'd have lunch," I say, trying not to sound as depressed as I feel.

He raises one eyebrow suspiciously. "Can't

today. I have an NJP in twenty minutes and I still have some TFOA reports to look over before the deployment," he apologizes.

A simple no would have sufficed. I knew what NJP was. Non-Judicial Punishment. Someone had been a bad monkey. But the other thing—

"TFOA report?" I ask.

"Things Falling Off Aircraft," he replies with a straight face.

"Seriously? Is that a frequent thing?" I laugh.

"You'd be surprised."

"So the deployment is still on schedule?" I ask.

"Yep, as of tomorrow, we will have the green light. We need to relieve VMAQ 135. They've been out over six months."

I knew when we got here that Dad would be deploying soon. If I don't find a friend to stay with while he's gone, I'll get shipped out to Kansas for six months to stay with Aunt P. The idea of spending the remainder of junior year in the K-12 school where she lives makes my brain hurt. No, I'll find somewhere else to go if it kills me.

"Dad, what did the hazmat guys say about the explosion in the paint room?" I press.

He looks at me, eyebrow raised. "I don't suppose you know anything about an email missing from my desk?"

I shrug, picking up the paperweight from his desk—an oversized gold Marine Corps ring—and play with it as I answer. "I might. I mean, I was just curious. Thought maybe I could get you some info about the sender."

"And did you?"

I shake my head, not meeting his eyes. "Nope, dead end."

He sighs. "Look, kid, I appreciate your naturally inquisitive nature, but leave the investigating to the professionals, okay?"

I frown. "That depends. Are they making any progress?"

"As a matter of fact, yes. The email account was one of those anonymous Hotmail accounts, but the IP address led them to the computer it was sent from. They expect to have a suspect in custody soon."

I roll my eyes. "I seriously doubt that."

"Why?"

"Because whoever sent it masked the IP through three different hosts, finally ending at a bulletproof server in China. They are chasing their tails." I look up. "I'm not saying they are slow, but I got all that in the first hour."

He just shakes his head. "Do you remember when you were little and we were stationed in 29 Palms?"

I think about it for a second. I'd been young then. Third or fourth grade, if I remember correctly. "Yes," I say hesitantly, wondering where this line of questioning is going.

"Do you remember when the youth center got vandalized? And you and the little boy from next door decided to catch the people doing it?"

I do remember that. His name was Darius, the boy from next door. He was a little younger than me, but we used to go to the youth center together after school to play games and make crafts. It was fun. Then somebody broke in and stole a bunch of stuff and spray painted the walls.

"What about it?" I ask, wondering why he's bringing that up now.

"You've always been one to try to figure things out, even then. You wanted to catch the bad guy." He pauses. "Puzzles, mysteries. You've always been a *solver*. A *fixer*. A *finder*. Do you remember what happened?"

Darius and I had snuck out our bedroom windows that night with flashlights, walkie-talkies, and my new camera. We spent most of the night crouched in a phone booth across the street from the youth center, waiting to see if the vandals showed up again. Which they did. I snapped a couple pictures, but they saw the flash and chased us all the way home. Only the angry barking of my Great Dane, Stormy, had convinced them not to chase us into my yard. I really miss that dog. He saved our bacon that night.

"As I recall, I solved that case for the police." I can't help but smirk.

He levels a heated gaze at me. "Yes, after being chased by three teenage boys who were more than willing to do you harm. You were extremely lucky that neither you nor that boy got hurt."

He has a point. Sort of.

I shake my head. "I'm not a little girl anymore, Dad."

"I know. But you know what they say about curiosity," he hints.

"I suppose it's a good thing I'm not of the feline persuasion then, huh?" I say, my chin in the air.

He leans back, his face resigned. "Did you find anything?" he asks, folding his arms across his chest.

"I'm not sure yet," I admit. "I thought I had the hacker thing pegged, but this thing last night, it kind of shoots holes in my theory. It would help if I had some info about the accident."

That's a minor exaggeration. I don't actually think it will help that much, but then, who knows? Maybe I'll see something no one else does.

He thinks about it for a minute, then pulls a manila folder out of his desk drawer and slides it over to me. "Here. This way you don't have to steal it," he says pointedly.

I cringe, flipping it open and reading his official report. When I finish, I have a few questions. "So there was no note this time? No email or anything?"

He shakes his head. "That's why we think it

might be an accident. But they found chemicals that we don't normally use. Unfortunately, it's all basic stuff, chemicals anyone could get online or in a hardware store. It could even have come in during that nightmare week when all the orders got so screwed up."

"Dad, who was on duty last night? In the guard shack and in the duty room?"

He evades my question. "If you're going to poke around, be subtle. The last thing I need is you inserting yourself into the middle of this mess any more than you already have."

"How hard is it to get in the paint room? I noticed some shops have keypads at the doors."

He shakes his head. "Nothing like that, just a door, and it's never locked in case one of the other shops needs to get in there for something," he answers. "Normally, there's always someone in there, but there was no weekend crew this week, so it was empty."

I stand up to leave.

"One more thing. Whoever was on duty last night would still be there today, for," he looks at his watch, "another two hours. It's a twenty-four hour shift."

I smile, mouth *thanks,* and leave, setting my now-empty cup on the counter by the door as I go. His clerk gives me a kind nod.

The duty shack is a dismal closet just off the ready room, which is where the flight crew meets before daily missions. At night, the duty guys usually watch TV or read to pass the time.

It would be pretty easy to sneak by without being seen, if you knew what you were doing. With no night crew on Saturdays, he was probably buys keeping himself occupied with other things. No use questioning him, I figure.

My main concern is the gate. In order to get into the building, you would need an ID card. The barcode on your ID unlocks the revolving gate and a record of everyone who comes through is logged in the security computer.

All these things are designed to keep the most advanced military squadron in the country secure. Somehow, someone has figured out how to beat the system. My plan is simple. Figure out how they got through security and I'll be one step closer to figuring out their identity.

According to Dad's file, no unauthorized personnel had entered the building that night, or at least none scanned their ID to get through the gate. I notice, as I leave, that the gate swings freely in the other direction. Someone could have snuck in some other way, but still got out here. It opens up some options.

In a well-lit parking lot, anyone trying to go over the gate would have been seen by someone. By my estimation, the bars on the turnstile are less than eight inches apart, so going through them is also out. The entire building is surrounded by a six-foot-tall fence with concertina wire looped along the top. Nasty stuff, way worse than barbed wire, which you could climb over just by draping a jacket over it. Concertina wire had tiny razor blades all over it.

I walk around the building, looking for any vulnerability in the fence. Hands in my pockets, T-shirt whipping in the breeze, I come to a small storage shack about five feet inside the fence. There's a beat-up white pickup truck parked parallel to it, in a no-parking zone.

A scenario runs through my brain. I scan the area for a streetlight. The nearest one is a few feet away, where I notice something on the black asphalt beneath it, reflecting in the sun.

I walk over to have a closer look. Broken glass. I kick some of it with the tip of my shoe before glancing up. The light has been broken out. Yeah, that'd make this area pretty hard to see in the dark. If it were nighttime, and if that truck, or one like it, was parked there, I could probably jump from the top of the cab to the roof of the shack, then hop down on the other side.

It would take someone fairly tall and athletic, someone with access to a truck.

It's Reid's voice in my head, whispering.

Someone like Oliver.

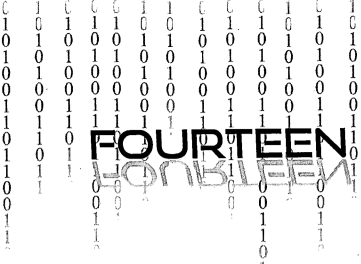

FOURTEEN

As I drive, I play scenarios over and over in my head. They all end the same way.

As if some kind of cosmic sign, Oliver's truck is parked outside my house when I get home. The cab is empty. I walk over, looking around for him, pulling myself up onto his running board to peer inside, then reluctantly, looking higher, at the roof. The top of his truck is spotless. Perfectly clean.

He probably washed it before the dance, I chastise myself.

Surely, if he'd stood on top of it, there'd be some kind of evidence. I jump down and walk to my front door. It's open a crack. I push it in, instantly feeling a deep, inexplicable wrongness to the situation.

I holler, "Hello?"

No answer.

But somewhere in my head, alarms are going off.

He's crazy, they shout. Amazing how the voices in my head have begun to sound like Reid.

I skirt along the entryway wall until I find

myself in the kitchen. I crouch down and maneuver myself over to the farthest drawer, sliding it open to find Dad's gun box. Using my thumbs, I enter the combination and it pops open, revealing a loaded Glock 9mm pistol. I take a deep breath. Maybe I'm just overreacting. But as a rule, it's better to be safe than sorry.

With the weapon tucked into my palm, I move slowly through the house, clearing each room as my father taught me. His words run through my head: *Two hands on the gun, arms pointing down, at the floor, safety off.*

Never point at anything you don't intend to shoot. Never shoot anything you don't intend to kill.

Lactic acid builds in my arms, shoulders, and back, making me tight and shaky. I take a few deep breaths to calm myself down as I go to my bedroom door. I press my back against the door and step in quickly. Oliver sits on my bed with his file in his hands, his head hung.

Shocked, I stand upright, taking one hand off the gun. "You stole my file," he whispers, finally looking up into my eyes.

The adrenaline pumps hard in my veins. "How did you get in here?" I demand.

The file falls from his hands, scattering papers on the floor. "The door was left open. I thought you might be hurt or something, so I let myself in. And I found that on your bed." He points at the folder at his feet.

Had I left the door cracked? That isn't like me at all. And the folder had been in my bag, I am sure of it.

"I can explain the file," I say. Well, no, I really can't. Not unless I admit I was looking into him as a suspect for the hacking.

In any case, he doesn't give me the chance.

"I don't want to hear it. I trusted you. I told you *everything*. What kind of person steals school files, anyway?"

He's angry, and rightfully so. I've invaded his privacy in a terrible, unforgiveable way.

He pushes past me and storms off. I want to call him back, to tell him how sorry I am, but I freeze. Torn somewhere between wanting to chase him, and being very relieved he is gone, I put the gun away.

I SPEND THE REST OF THE DAY IN MY ROOM, STEWING. When I pick Kayla up for school on Monday, it still isn't any better. It feels like I'm juggling, always too many balls in the air, always a half second from everything falling down on top of me.

We sit for a while in the car in front of Kayla's house. She fiddles with the black rosary around her wrist. Her purple cheetah-print tank top is almost the same shade she'd dyed her hair on Sunday. With her tall, black boots and fishnet stockings under a suspiciously short skirt, she's four feet, eleven inches of pure attitude.

"I warned you about that boy," she points out after I finish banging my head into the steering wheel as I spill my problems. "You shoulda picked Reid. He's a good guy. But no, you had to go for the psychopath. You have a thing for the wrong kind of right, don't you?"

I frown, mostly because it's true. My history with guys sucks.

Sitting back, I close my eyes. The worst part is, my suspicions mean nothing. I know deep down that Oliver had nothing to do with any of this. I'm sure about it, and I can't even explain why.

I feel a fraction better, having vented, but the ache is still there. "What am I gonna do, Kayla?" A frantic horror overtakes me. "I don't even know where I'm gonna stay during the deployment. I'd rather live in a box under the bridge than go back to my aunt's place."

"You can stay with me," she offers, "We have a spare bedroom since my big bro left for boot camp. Derek crashes in it sometimes. It's free if you need it."

I'm touched by her offer. Staying with Kayla will be great, if her parents really don't mind.

"Oh my God, that would be amazing. Maybe I should come over sometime and meet your folks," I suggest.

"Sure. My mom works from home, so whenever is fine," she says, pulling her magenta locks into a messy bun on the top of her head. "And as far as the boy drama, just take a breather. Sit back and let the dust clear for a while."

I nod, knowing that not only is she right, but there's nothing else I can do.

When we get to Derek's, he's less than thrilled about the idea of me spending the deployment with Kayla.

"Where will I stay?" he whines.

I know he is worried about losing his hideout for when things get rough at his house. It reminds me of something else I've been meaning to do.

She pats him on the leg. "No worries. We still have a perfectly cozy couch."

Reid is quiet when I pick him up. I wasn't even sure I should, but I'd have felt worse if I didn't at least make an effort. Sure enough, he's outside waiting for me when I arrive. His eyes are dark, like he hasn't slept, and his face pale. And though I don't expect it, he is holding two white sacks from the bakery. When he slips into the car, he hands me a donut. I smile, but he looks away. It's a simple gesture. We're still friends, even though we're fighting right now. It makes a small part of my heart swell. At least I haven't completely destroyed everything. Yet.

When we get to school, I walk beside him into

the building. "Look, Reid. I wanted to say I'm sorry about the other day."

"No, it's my fault. I shouldn't have come down on you like that," he offers.

"Yep, we both suck. However, if you still feel up to being my wing man, I have an idea," I say slyly.

He shakes his head full of dark, unruly hair and grins. "What do you need?"

FIFTEEN

A T LUNCH, I SIT BESIDE CASSY, WHO IS TALKING IN excited tones with Bianca. They are obviously rehashing something they'd watched over the weekend and are so absorbed in conversation they don't seem to notice me sit down across from them.

"Hey guys, have a good weekend?" I ask, taking a bite of my chicken parmesan sandwich, catching a drip of marinara with my tongue as it leaks out the side of my mouth.

Cassy turns to me, only to catch sight of Reid entering the cafeteria behind me. Her eyes dart up and lock on like lasers. "Oh, you know. Girls' night."

"Sorry I missed it."

"How was the dance?" Bianca asks, tucking a strand of blonde hair behind her ear.

I smile. "Really good. It was my first real school dance so..."

"Did you cry in the bathroom?" she asks, leaning toward Cassy. "I've always said, it's not a party until someone's crying in the bathroom."

"No, thankfully. And the only zombies that showed up were the chaperones." I snap my fingers in an *aw shucks* gesture. "Maybe next year."

"There's always prom," Cassy says, her voice light and wistful, her eyes still locked on Reid.

"You should ask him," I say quietly. "I bet he'd say yes."

Her eyes flicker back down to me, her cheeks flushing. She shakes her head. "Call me old fashioned, but I want to be asked to prom by someone who actually wants to be there with me and not someone else," she says pointedly.

I frown but try to ignore the jab. "That reminds me, Reid is coming over to help me study for the chemistry midterm; you guys wanna come over too? It won't take long, an hour tops, and I'll spring for pizza?"

Cassy agrees first, Bianca finally nodding too.

"Sure, why not?"

BY THE TIME BIANCA ARRIVES, CASSY AND REID ARE already in the living room, sitting on the floor, devouring the first still-hot slices of pepperoni and pineapple pizza.

"Glad you could come," I say, waving her in.

She takes a seat next to Cassy and pulls her laptop from her bag. I open my tablet, and Reid slides his laptop over to Cassy. I nod for him to begin.

"Ok, so I thought the best way to do it would be a quick practice test. I've sent you each an email with ten questions. Once you finish the test, pass your computer to the right and we will score each other. Sound good?" he explains.

"Works for me," I say, stuffing a bite of pizza in my mouth. "The Wi-Fi password is zero, P-E-N, at symbol, T-H-E-C-L, zero, S+E."

He takes out his phone and sets the timer. "Let me know once you have the email open and we'll start. Since the midterm is timed, I'm going to give us fifteen minutes to finish."

"Ok, I'm ready," Cassy says.

"Me too," Bianca adds.

"Shoot," I mutter around the scalding cheese in my mouth.

I open the test email, add the answers from the key in my note file, then open another window, following the wireless link from my Wi-Fi and into Bianca's hard drive. Plugging the discreet jump drive into my USB port, I run the program that will sift through her recent Internet history and retrieve her username and password from the Omega Portal site.

It takes exactly fourteen and a half minutes.

Files found and saved, I remove the drive, close the secondary window, and pass my test and answers to Cassy, taking Bianca's computer and grading her score.

She missed half the questions.

Once we're done studying and eating, Bianca and Cassy head out, Reid staying behind to help me clean up.

"So, did you get what you needed?" he asks, tossing a small stack of paper plates in the trash can.

I nibble at my bottom lip before answering. "Yes and no. Here's what's not making sense to me. Say she's the hacker—a total possibility—then why not just stick to that? Why suddenly change things up and go into the squadron directly? It's risky at best. Plus, not only do I doubt she knows her way around chemicals enough to pull it off, but she has an alibi for the night it happened."

He frowns, pushing his glasses up the bridge of his nose. "What are you saying?"

I shake my head. "I'm saying that either she didn't do it at all, or maybe there are two suspects. One, a hacker looking to cause trouble, and another, willing to get their hands dirty and risk really hurting someone."

I toss the empty cardboard box on the kitchen counter, retrieving a fresh trash bag from the bottom drawer.

"You think someone else set the explosion in the paint room."

I nod. "Yeah, I do. Bianca is many things, but at the end of the day, I just don't think she'd deliberately hurt someone."

"So why did you need to get into her computer?" he asks.

"Because, if she did hack the squadron, there'll be a trail. I need to know if she did—and why she did—before I go to anyone about it. I know what it's like when one rash, impulsive decision ruins your whole life. I'm not willing to put that on her if it was some kind of prank or desperate move that went too far. Especially if she's not the one who set up the explosion. Now, if it's more than that, if she's serious about selling the hack or something, I'll take what I have and hand it over to the authorities."

He nods. "That's fair, I suppose. What about the person who set up the explosion?'

I rake my fingers through my hair, tugging on the strands as frustration bubbles under my skin. "I honestly don't know. I think I know how they got into and out of the building, but that's it. It's worse than nothing."

He puts a hand on my shoulder. "Hey, let's focus on what we can do, and leave the rest to the authorities."

I nod, patting his hand.

"Hey, on the upside, Kayla's mom said I could stay with them during the deployment," I offer, trying to perk myself up.

"That's cool," he says. "Once my parents are gone, I'll have my house all to myself. We'll have to throw a raging party."

I feel myself laugh. "In that house? They'd kill you."

He shrugs. "What they don't know can't hurt me. Besides, I gotta do something. Being on my own for that long gets old fast."

Now it's my turn to comfort him. I hand him the last can of soda, raising my own in a toast. "To those of us left behind."

He smiles, tapping the cans together.

After taking him home I head to Kayla's house. Her mother, Mae, is a petite Korean woman, a seamstress who makes extra cash mending uniforms and sewing patches and things for the personnel. Kayla's dad, Staff Sergeant Pierce, works in the Rapids office making IDs and stuff. Their house is cozy with an Asian flair, with lots of brass knickknacks and beautifully elaborate paintings. Kayla's bedroom walls are plastered with posters for various bands, with one entire wall dedicated to pictures of her and Derek, all taped together into a massive collage. Her bed is small, twin size, with neon-green bedding. The floor is littered with papers, clothes, and Hot Pockets wrappers, and there's a powerful scent of lavender incense in the air.

"This is where you'll be staying," Mae says, opening the adjacent door.

The guest room is a warm, latte-brown with brightly colored fans on the wall. The bed is small, like Kayla's, but with a rich, chocolate-brown coverlet and off-white sheets. Her mom seems excited about the idea of me staying with them for a few months. I offer up some extra cash to help with household expenses while I stay there, a condition from my father, but she refuses.

"No, no. Don't even think of it." She smiles warmly before turning to chase a puffy, white cat down the hall.

I get the impression that Kayla and her family like to take in strays. Kayla's cat, Morpheus, is curled up on the spare bed. She's a ratty-looking creature with one eye and long, matted, ginger fur, but that doesn't keep Kayla from picking the poor feline up and snuggling her.

I don't stay long. Dad texts to say he's on his way home and I really want to catch him before he turns in for the night. With a hug and a promise to come again soon, Mae releases me, and Kayla walks me to the door.

When I arrive home, Dad is just pulling in. I catch him outside his sedan and we walk inside together.

"So what have you been up to?" he asks, opening the front door.

"Kayla's mom wanted to give me the tour. She's really sweet. I think it'll be good," I say, stepping inside and flipping the light switch.

"That's great, kid," he says, stripping off his jacket

and draping it over a kitchen chair. "Any pizza left?" he asks, poking at the empty box. "There's a game on I wanna watch."

"No, sorry. I can go pick something up for you or make you a sandwich."

He waves me off. "I'm good. I'll have some leftovers."

I shift my weight from left to right and back again, the jump drive in my pocket beginning to burn a hole in my brain. "I need to go study. You sure you don't need anything?"

He leans down headfirst in the fridge. "I can feed myself, you know."

I shrug. "It's your health."

Heading to the office, I grab my tablet from my bag, setting it to charge on the desk beside me as I plug in the jump drive and start opening files. Once I have the log-in info, I pull up the Omega Portal and log in as Bianca, backtracking through the history. Sure enough, Splice has a private email account deep in the corner of the dark web. I open it, logging back through sent files. There, deleted but not erased, is the email to my dad. I scroll back further and find another email; this sent to a series of social media profiles.

That's how they got into the system. They sent it around on September eleventh, a jpeg file of an eagle superimposed on a patriotic message. It got passed around social sites, ending up in some random email. When opened inside the UNIX mainframe, it released a hidden Trojan that hacked the system. I open the code, looking at the design. The code itself is elegant, both subtle and fierce. Normal virus blockers wouldn't even pick it up. Then there's another section of code, and it's so far beyond me, I can't even tell what it's designed to do.

Then it clicks into place. It's an Ouroboros virus. I've heard of them but never seen the guts of one. It slithers into the system through the security cracks, creates a back door into the system, and then eats itself before anyone can discover it.

Well, it's not a surprise, really. That's how I would have done it.

From there, I begin back tracing all the chat and private messaging activity. There's very little. As Bianca had said, the most recent chats are all in forums with people looking to buy and sell their virginity. The chats seem harmless, research, as she'd claimed. I go back further. There's no chatter about the squadron, nothing about buying or selling viruses or anything of the sort. But something does flag red. It's a series of random videos. I click the first one.

The screen fills with images of flaming wreckage. A tall, slender reporter speaking in solemn tones.

"There is no confirmation yet, but it's believed that three Army servicemen perished in the wreck," he says as the flames behind him lick skyward.

I click the second. It's a piece of a horror movie from the late seventies. I recognize one of the actresses creeping down the stairs, a bright red fire axe in her hand.

When I click the third, my heart drops into my stomach. It's a grainy web video of my dad's office. I recognize the photo on the wall behind his chair. The room is empty, as far as I can tell, but as I keep watching, Dad's assistant comes in, sets a stack of papers next to his keyboard, and walks out. A few more minutes pass and Dad comes into frame. With one burly hand, he pulls his chair out and takes a seat. He takes a sip of coffee and starts hammering at the keyboard, completely unaware that he's being recorded by his own webcam. There are dozens of other videos, each various work station computers inside the building.

The screen goes dark and a wave of dread washes over me.

Bianca—Splice—may not be selling secrets, but we need to have a very serious conversation.

Then something else dawns on me. If I hand this over, innocent prank or not, the NSA or some other alphabet agency is going to scoop her up and put her somewhere she may never see daylight again.

My hands hover over the keyboard. If I delete it, then what? Even if they trace it back, there's nothing to find at that point. How much am I willing to risk to protect someone I'm not even sure if I like?

SIXTEEN

THOUGH I CLOSE THE COMPUTER AND GO TO BED, I don't sleep. I spend the night tossing and turning, my mind racing a thousand miles an hour. Un-rested but somehow still alert, I dress and head to school the next morning, a double espresso in a white paper cup in hand as I pick up my group.

"Long night?" Derek asks. "Or did you lose a fight with your eyeliner?"

I smirk humorlessly. "Decided to go for heroin sheik today."

He grins. "It works for you."

I salute him with my espresso and take a sip, maneuvering one handed into a parking spot.

By second period, I'm crashing, doodling absently in my notebook when a shrill, earsplitting alarm rings through the air.

"Okay, class. Don't panic. Gather your things and head to the gym. No pushing!" My teacher, Mr. White, ushers us from the room.

I scoop up my books and toss them into my bag.

In the hall, Reid grabs me by the arm, offering me a look that's part concern, part determination.

We veer left, down the hall, ducking into an alcove as a group of students pass. Checking to make sure the hall is clear, we head away from the gym and toward the parking lot.

"Where are we going?" I ask as we slip outside through the west doors unnoticed.

"To your car. We need to get out of here," he whispers urgently. "I want to make sure our parents are all right, and you drove."

"Farris!"

I spin around when I hear my name from across the parking lot. "Oliver, what are you doing?" I ask as he jogs up to me.

He hasn't paid any attention to me for days, opting instead to give me a well-deserved cold shoulder. What can he possibly want now?

Reid steps between us. "We don't have time for this right now, Oliver," he challenges, spitting out the name like it's a bad word.

"I need to talk to Farris," he answers, pushing Reid to the side. "It's none of your business."

Before I realize what's going on, Reid grabs Oliver's arm and twists it around, pinning it to his back.

"Don't push me," Reid threatens, his face a twisting mask of hatred. I'd never seen that look on Reid's face before and I'm not quite sure how to react.

He drops Oliver's arm and pushes him forward. Oliver turns, his arm drawing back as if he's about to throw a punch, when I step between them.

"That's enough!" I shout, pulling Oliver away.

"Reid, wait for me in the car. I'll just be a minute."

He huffs but does as he's told. I tug Oliver's arm until we stand a few feet away.

"What is it?" I ask, trying not to let my annoyance creep into my voice.

"Don't go," he begs, his eyes pleading.

In some dizzy daydream, this would be the part where he forgives me and I throw myself into his arms, letting him kiss me until everything is alright again. But his next words shatter the illusion.

"At least, not with him."

That's it. A deep-seated rage boils inside me. I don't know if he ever really liked me or if it is just some stupid contest between them, but I'm done with it.

I point into the air. "Those sirens, that's the sound of my dad, of his parents, possibly being hurt or worse. And you're going to step up to me, after throwing shade at me for days, and give me some macho crap about not leaving with my friend?" I pause to lick my lips, a well-deserved look of regret washing across his face. "This is me, being completely done with you."

When I walk away, I don't look back. But some

small, sad part of me really wants to.

WE DRIVE STRAIGHT TO THE SQUADRON. IT'S A testament to the fact that all the MPs are occupied that I don't get a speeding ticket as I race through the mostly empty streets. My engine roars as we fly across the base, as if my anxiety has leached through the vinyl seats and straight into the injectors.

Bright-yellow Crash Fire Rescue trucks sit scattered throughout the parking lot, their lights flashing. Someone has cut the wire fence to allow emergency personnel in and out without having to squeeze through the turnstile. Marines, both enlisted and officers, congregate in the parking lot, spilling onto the flight line. The smoke is thin and quickly blowing away with the breeze, but even as I pull in and slam on my brakes, I see what's happened. The right side of the building is collapsed, the mangled steel and brick mixing in a kaleidoscope of flaming wreckage. I'm out of the car before the engine even dies, sprinting through the chaos. I get as far as the front gate before a pair of arms grabs me, holding me back.

"Miss, you can't go in there!" the voice belonging to the arms yells over the chaos.

I struggle against his vice grip on my arm. "My dad's in there!"

Two more guards rush over to help restrain me.

My mind reels, scanning the crowd for a glimpse of my father and finding none.

Time slows down around me. My pulse beats wildly in my own ears, blocking out the sirens and the voices of the men holding me. It's a familiar, disconnected feeling, as if I'm outside the scene, looking in, detached from what's going on around me. Out of the corner of my eye, I see Reid talking to a man in yellow firefighter pants, his face blank. In a rush of sound, time catches up with itself and the hysteria floods back in.

"You need to go back to your car, ma'am," the guard is telling me. "You can't be here."

A familiar woman shuffles up to me, her khaki uniform singed and blackened in places, her red curls disheveled. The admin clerk from Dad's office.

"Miss Barnett?" she asks.

I stop struggling. She waves her hand, and the guard releases me.

"Where's my father?" I demand, my voice sharp and penetrating.

"The Lieutenant Colonel was taken to the hospital with minor injuries," she says. "The crash..." she hesitates, glancing back over her shoulder. "The pilots ejected safely. No one was in the area of the building that took the most damage."

Spots burst into my vision. I clutch at her shirt to keep myself from falling. She misunderstands my movement and pulls me into a hug, stroking my hair like a child.

"He's okay?" I push the words through my constricted throat before pulling away. Her red curls feel like steel wool on my face.

She chokes back a sob, taking a deep, rattling breath as she speaks. "We were going to a meeting in Maintenance Control. Your father wanted to go through the hangar and see how some drop tank repairs were going. As soon as he opened the door, the building shook. A steel rafter came down; it missed him but caught the door. It slammed back and hit him pretty hard. He was bleeding..." She trails off, as if realizing she shouldn't be saying any of this to me.

I grab her by her upper arms, shaking her hard. "You're sure he's okay?"

She seems to focus, visibly pulling herself together. "He was unconscious, but stable when they took him out."

Before I can ask anything else, an EMT throws a wool blanket over her shoulders and leads her away to an ambulance, slipping an oxygen mask over her face. She shoots me a concerned look over her shoulder as she walks away.

I glance back at the building just in time to see two firefighters in full gear running through the door. They're shouting something I can't make out. Less than a heartbeat later, a loud boom that rocks the whole parking lot knocks me onto the ground.

I watch as a cloud of dense black smoke rises into the sky. I can't hear anything for a minute but the beating of my own pulse in my ears. When the sound comes back with a *pop,* I get up, looking around in a daze.

As I watch, one of the fire crew pulls off his helmet and yells, "Another wall went down, south side of the building. It's pretty unstable back there."

I run across the street and back to my car, where Reid is already waiting for me, leaning against my door.

"Are your parents all right?" I ask sliding into the car.

"Yeah. They were in the air, but this wasn't one of theirs. They've been rerouted to Seymour Johnson Air Force Base. I'll probably hear from them soon," he says, looking calmer than I feel as he slides into the passenger seat.

I clutch the wheel with white, trembling fingers. The scrapes on my palms ache from where I tried to break my fall. Grit clings to the flesh. I'm bleeding, I can tell, but I refuse to look. My eyes go in and out of focus, the window in front of me going blurry as I try to focus past it, to the street ahead. I blink back the tears. Reid reaches over, trying to clutch my hands with his own, but I jerk them away and tuck them between my legs.

"Your dad?" he asks softly.

I shake my head, trying to bring myself out of

the panicked state I've slipped into. "At the hospital. I need to go see him. You want me to drop you at home on the way?" And just like that, the world snaps back into focus like a rubber band releasing itself. Suddenly, my brain is processing at full speed, every synapse firing in a chaotic stream. I take a deep breath, close my eyes, and count to five, knowing that if I don't get myself under control, I'll hyperventilate and pass out.

"Why don't you let me drive you to the hospital?" Reid offers, keeping his voice calm. "I'll walk from there; it's not far."

I look up at him and see the concern in his expression. Catching a glimpse of myself in the rearview mirror, I understand why. My cheeks are flushed, my eyes wide and wild. Stray strands of hair hang from my disheveled ponytail and there's a smudge of soot on my chin.

"It's ok," I say firmly, as if trying to force myself to believe it. "I'm ok. Just buckle up."

He'll be fine, I tell myself over and over in my head as we pull out onto the street, tires squealing against the pavement.

He has to be.

SEVENTEEN

THE ON-BASE HOSPITAL IS LIKE ANY OTHER: COLD, sterile, and smelling vaguely of bleach cleaner. The corpsman at the front desk is supremely unhelpful when I arrive, already short on patience and half looking for a fight.

The thing I hate most about hospitals is the surprising lack of urgency. Everyone moves with a deliberateness that's completely infuriating when your heart is racing and your panic rising. Call me crazy, but it would make me feel a bit better to see at least one person who seems to be as freaked out as I am. But no, the man, probably in his late twenties and already balding enough to be very noticeable, just sits there in his white uniform, telling me to calm down. Someone will be with me soon.

The only thing that keeps me from going over the crescent-shaped desk is Reid's hand on my shoulder.

After half an hour of sitting in the stiff waiting room chair, which feels like an eternity, the doctor finally appears. He isn't wearing the green scrubs you see on TV; rather, he has on a white lab coat over a khaki uniform. When he calls my last name, it's in a flat, dull voice like having your number called at the DMV.

I stand anxiously, wiping my hands down the back of my jeans. "That's me. How's my dad?"

He motions with his metal clipboard for me to follow him. "He's doing fine. You can see him now."

Reid stands. "If you're ok, I'm gonna head home and wait for my parents to call and check in."

I nod. "Yeah, I'm good. Thanks for staying with me."

He presses his lips together. "If you need anything, just call."

As the doctor leads me to Dad's room, I exhale as if I've been holding my breath for hours, letting the tension bleed from my neck and shoulders. *Of course he's okay*, I chide myself. It'll take a lot more than a little explosion to take the Lieutenant Colonel down. The doctor shows me to a wall with a large, glass window overlooking the bed where my dad lays, looking smaller and frailer than I've ever thought possible. He's hooked up to a bunch of tubes and wires and has a white bandage across his forehead. A shiver dances up my back and into my neck.

"Your father was extremely lucky. The ER is full of people injured in the crash. It's a miracle no one died," the doctor says, making a quick note on Dad's chart before continuing. "All in all, it's a concussion, some bumps and bruises. But we're going to keep him at least overnight for observation." With that, he turns, leaving me to my visit.

Dad's eyes are closed when I creep into his room. My shoes squeak on the heavily waxed, beige linoleum floor, waking him.

"Hey, kid," he says, struggling to prop himself awkwardly on one elbow.

Grabbing a stool from the far corner of the room, I roll it to the bedside, sitting down and resting my arms on the metal rails of his bed. "Hey, Dad. How're you feeling?" I ask, fidgeting with the cord that runs from his index finger to a pulse monitor, making sure it's not stuck under one of my wheels.

"Kind of like I've been hit by a plane, which is appropriate, I suppose. Or at least I did. The meds are kicking in now." His words slur a bit. It should be funny, but it's just the opposite. Seeing him like this is terrifying, chilling me deep in my bones.

I'm glad he isn't in pain, at least, though the beeping of the monitors make me grind my teeth. These are the sounds I hear in my nightmares, the last sounds I heard before Mom died.

"What happened?" I ask, pulling the white blanket up over his chest as he lay back down.

"It's all fuzzy. I was down in Maintenance Control talking to Sergeant Gomez. I remember opening the door to the hangar bay, a flash of light, then nothing..." His voice trails off as he slips back into sleep.

I pat his hand, careful not to disturb the IV, and kiss his forehead, avoiding the large, square patch of gauze taped over his right eye. Then I just sit beside him for a while, watching him sleep and sending silent prayers of thanks to the heavens that he's all right. I'm not sure how long I sit there, but when I stand up, my back aches. I switch off the light over his bed, plunging the room into semidarkness. Closing the door quietly behind me, I flag down the nurse at the desk outside.

"He's sleeping." I motion to Dad's door.

"That's probably a good thing," he says. "He had a nasty bump on the head, a few minor scrapes, and a broken rib. Your father was very lucky today. Four other injured personnel had to be flown to Bethesda."

I nod, thank him again, and head out.

I bite my lip as I walk out the front glass doors and into the sunshine. I should go confront Bianca, force her to turn herself in. Pulling my phone from my wallet, I look at the time It's after five already. Bianca will have to wait till tomorrow. As it is, the squadron is frozen. What more could anyone do now? At least my dad, banged up as he is, is safe. Besides, I'm still feeling shaky, and there's really only one person I want to see tonight.

I'M NOT A HUNDRED PERCENT SURE THIS IS A GOOD idea. Hell, I'm not *one* percent sure, but I drive anyway. *I should just go home*, I keep telling myself. But somehow, the idea of facing the dark house, of spending the night alone, feels... impossible.

Half in a daze, I don't realize I've made up my mind until I pull into Oliver's driveway. Georgia is in the front yard, checking the tires on her powder-blue Prius.

"Hey," she says with warmth in her voice. Her face falls into a concerned pucker.

"Hey," I say back, my voice on the edge of cracking.

"How's your dad?" she asks gently, scooping me into a tight hug before I can stop her.

Hold it together, I tell myself, digging my fingernails into the palms of my hands until I can feel the crescent-shaped indentations forming in my skin. It hurts—not badly, but enough to help me focus.

"Dad's fine. He's in the hospital, but he's ok." I clench my jaw, speaking through my teeth. "Is Oliver here?"

She releases me, jerking her head toward the house, "In his room, you can go on in."

I hear the music emanating from his bedroom as soon as I'm in the house. Punk rock, probably Green Day, if I had to guess. As I get closer, I distinguish a thumping rhythm that doesn't fit the beat. I knock gently.

"Oliver?" I call over the music. "It's me. Farris."

The thumping stops and the volume drops to almost nothing. He opens the door, leaning on it with a small basketball in his free hand. "What are you doing here?" he asks, his voice every bit as irritated as I deserve.

I open my mouth to talk, to apologize or beg forgiveness or something, anything, but nothing comes out.

A massive tear rolls down my cheek. I mouth *I'm sorry*, but no sound comes out.

Dropping the ball without hesitation, Oliver pulls me into his arms. He guides us to the edge of his bed and sits us down with me sobbing into his shoulder. I nuzzle into the curve of his neck, inhaling him between sobs. How is it that with all the lies and all the disappointments between us that he can still feel like this, like the only solid thing in the entire universe?

He strokes my hair, saying nothing. His arms are solid, but loose enough to let me breathe freely, strong enough to keep me from falling apart completely.

"I'm going to take five minutes to totally freak out. Is that okay?" I ask weakly.

He tightens his grip just a little. "Take whatever you need."

I know at that moment that I love him. It's crazy and messy and hard, but there it is. Neither of us is perfect, but maybe, just maybe, we are perfect for each other. And maybe, if it's easy, it's not real.

When Mom got sick, I'd been the one holding her. I cooked dinner for Dad, made sure the house was taken care of, went with Mom to her appointments... all that had fallen to me. Dad couldn't deal with it, so I had to step up and be strong. Maybe part of me grew arrogant in that strength, in the idea that I didn't need anyone, that I could handle anything.

But I was wrong. The idea of losing Dad shakes me in ways I don't want to admit. Rationally, I know he's okay, but for some reason, I just can't get a grip on myself. So I lean on Oliver, and thankfully, he lets me.

Once the worst of it has run its course, I wipe my eyes with the back of my hand and pull away. Oliver looks into my eyes, his expression gentle, concerned. I almost start crying again.

No, I tell myself, *time's up*. Gotta pull it together. Compose myself. There's so much I want to say, and if I don't do it now, I'll lose the courage.

"I'm sorry," I whisper. "The last time I was in a hospital, it was to be with my mom before she died. Seeing my dad in there, it was just..." I hold my hands up in surrender.

There are no words.

He wipes my cheek with his thumb. "Is he going

to be okay?"

I nod, sniffling.

Pulling me back to him, he hugs me tightly. "I'm here if you need me. You don't have to be strong all the time. I can be strong for you sometimes, if you want me to," he offers.

Without thinking, I turn my face up and kiss him. It's gentle at first—I half expect him to push me away—but quickly grows urgent. Desperate. I can't breathe, so tightly is his mouth on mine, and I can't make myself care. My lungs burn, but it seems like such a small fire compared to all the others that rage inside me. How can anyone survive this? It's like being consumed, every cell of my body aching in ways I never imagined.

When he pulls away, we both gasp for air like we'd been drowning. Laughing awkwardly, I lean back on my hands.

He growls, "You're killing me Farris."

I bite my bottom lip, scraping skin with my teeth. "Listen, Ollie, about the file. I'm so sorry. I know it was wrong to look at it without asking you first. I was looking into some weird stuff happening at the squadron".

"And you thought I might be behind it?" he cuts me off.

I shake my head. "No. I didn't even ask for your file. Reid just sort of dropped it in my lap."

"Of course he did," he mutters, leaning forward,

touching his forehead to mine.

"But I did hack the school computer to pull files on all the kids with parents in or attached to the squadron," I admit. "I thought if I could figure out who had motive, I could find out who was behind it all."

"So you thought one of us was behind all this?" he asks.

I close my eyes. "Yeah, I still do."

He hesitates. "I'm glad you told me. I just want to get to a place where we can be completely honest with each other."

I swallow, knowing there's more I need to get off my chest. "I want that too. So, here I go," I say. "Everything you want to know about Farris and some things you didn't."

He listens patiently as I tell him everything. Starting with what happened at my old school, my mom's death, and ending with every snippet of what I had found online. I tell him about hacking the email, the Omega Portal, Splice, everything.

When I finish, it's late and his room is dark. We're lying side by side on his bed, and I'm curled into his chest, listening to his heartbeat. It's slow, steady, and calming.

"Thank you," he whispers, kissing the top of my head.

I nod, all talked out. Part of me wonders if I should leave, if his parents will be upset that I'm here so late, but I let those thoughts fade away with each thump... thump... thump.

Above us, the ceiling fan spins, stirring the air so gently, it almost feels like being outside.

"If you are determined to look into this, I can help you," he offers.

Intrigued, I prop myself up on my elbow. "What do you mean?"

"Well," he says thoughtfully. "You're thinking that Bianca just got in over her head with a prank, that maybe someone else did the other stuff, right?"

I nod.

"What if it's easier than that? What if she told someone about the prank, or someone found it on her computer, and they decided to jump on board? Maybe she knows who it is. If she told someone about it, who would she tell?"

I feel the name on my lips like sour candy. "Cassy."

"It's a place to start at least. I say talk to Bianca, make her come clean." He reaches over, squeezing my hand. "We'll figure it out," he says. "I promise."

EIGHTEEN

"I SHOULD GO," I MANAGE WEAKLY.

He kisses me on the forehead. "You could stay. My mom's off visiting my aunt and dad will be stuck on shift till dawn."

I groan. The offer is so tempting, much, much too tempting. But I shake my head. "I'm going to go check on Dad, and then I need to get home." Lowering my head, I kiss him until I'm rethinking my words.

I make it back to the hospital before two am. Dad's still sleeping deeply, thanks to whatever's in his IV. I convince a friendly corpsman to give him a message that I've gone home and will be back in the morning.

The house is dark and still when I step inside, locking the bolt behind me. Overcome with exhaustion, emotional as well as physical, I crawl into my bed, clothes still on, and pass out.

A loud knock on the front door wakes me just after seven. I drag myself out of bed to find Kayla on the other side of it. Her black hair is streaked with blue, a shiny silver ring in her bottom lip as she greets me with a smile.

Still only half awake, I reach out and flick the tiny piercing. "Is that real?"

She slaps my hand away. "Yes. Leave it alone. It still stings."

She steps into the hallway, closing the door behind her. I smell something sweet but before I can ask, she holds out a white foam carton, popping the lid open to expose two of the largest, gooiest-looking cinnamon rolls I've ever seen.

"How's your dad?" she asks, brushing past me and into the kitchen where she scoops the pastries onto paper plates.

I yawn and scratch my head before answering. "He's fine. I'm heading over there today to see him. Shouldn't you be at school?"

She raises an eyebrow. I must look confused because she steps past me into my living room and switches on the TV. She flips a few channels, settling on one, turns up the volume and motions for me to look.

"Base schools are closed today in the wake of a devastating plane crash at the new Joint Strike Fighter squadron VMX 195 that resulted in over a dozen confirmed injuries."

I stare at the TV, my mouth hanging open. This was not something that made it to the news, especially not before the investigation was over.

The female news anchor continues. "According to an unnamed source, a suspect is in custody. Due to his age, we cannot release his name at this time, but sources tell News Channel 7 he is a student at Cherry Point High School."

Stunned, I turn to Kayla and manage to form one word, "Who?"

She shifts uncomfortably and sits down, motioning for me to do the same. "The MPs found a bunch of chemicals in the back of Oliver's truck this morning. They arrested him. I guess someone saw him steal the stuff from the lab at school and called the police with an anonymous tip."

I fall into the chair beside her, shaking my head. *No*. It can't be Oliver. There is no doubt in my mind now, no moment of hesitation. Just a firm certainty I can't explain. Part of me wants to scream, to call Kayla a liar and proclaim Oliver's innocence, but the words stick in my throat. No, something else is going on, I can feel it.

But can I prove it?

NINETEEN

I SHOWER AND DRESS BEFORE KAYLA CAN POLISH OFF even one of the cinnamon rolls. As for me, mine sits untouched. My appetite is the last thing on my mind right now. She's still standing at the counter, hunched over her breakfast, when I come in, tossing my backpack on the kitchen table.

"What's up?" she mumbles around a bite.

I stuff my phone, tablet, and lock-pick set into the empty sack. "Oliver didn't do this."

She frowns, sticking the fork in the remains of her breakfast. "Look, Farris, I know you like this guy, but he's obviously guilty. I mean, Reid says they found the same chemicals in his truck that set off that explosion last week."

"And what about the crash? He was at school when it happened. We all were."

"Reid says he probably messed with the plane when he set up the explosion." She shrugs. "Oliver's got major problems, Farris. You know that."

Ignoring her comment, I grab my keys. "Where

is he? Oliver? Do you know?"

She wiggles her lip ring with her tongue before answering. "At his house, I think. I did a drive by. There were a bunch of MP jeeps in the driveway. Probably holding him there until Homeland can get someone out here to question him. He's a minor, so they can't really just toss him in jail." She pauses. "Either that, or they'll take him to the Provost Marshal's office. It's in that plaza where the housing office is."

I nod, vaguely familiar with the area. Closing the flap on my bag, I sling it over my head and across my body. "You want a ride somewhere?" I ask.

She shakes her head, purple curls bouncing. "Nah. I'll walk home."

There's no way this ends well, I realize. Even if I go to them with everything I have, it might not be enough to clear Oliver, of setting the explosion at least. The crash, however, I might be able to shed some light on. Reaching forward in an unexpected rush of emotion, I hug her quickly.

"Thanks for everything, Kayla."

She hugs me back, feeling like a doll in my arms, small, fragile, and in need of protection. "Good luck."

First, I drive by Oliver's house. There are no jeeps at all, though the entire area is taped off in yellow plastic tape, a single MP watching as a tow truck driver loads Oliver's truck onto the back of a flat bed, so I drive on. As soon as I arrive at the

Marshal's office, I know there's no way I'm getting in there. I dial Oliver's phone, but it goes straight to voice mail.

Knowing I'll most likely be in a shit load of trouble for this, I park and pull out my tablet. It takes me almost fifteen minutes to hack into the building security cameras. In the grainy black and white, I spot him.

Oliver sits alone, handcuffed to the wooden arm of the off-white sofa. His hair is tousled, as I'd left it, and deep, dark bags sit under his eyes. He's slumped forward as far as the cuffs will allow. The rest of the room is empty, but I see a small, rectangular window above his head, steel bars seeming redundant since it's barely six inches tall, less than a foot across. Still, it's my best bet.

I log off and tuck my tablet away. Slipping out of the car, I walk casually along the sidewalk until I can see the rear of the building, a set of tiny, barred windows. Making a quick beeline for them, I scoop up a small rock, rise up to my tiptoes, and tap on the glass with it, which has a small corner already missing.

"Oliver, you ok?" I ask. "Don't turn around, there are cameras. Just stay still like nothing is happening."

"You gonna break me out?" He chuckles, and it's a sad, ominous sound.

"I'd bake you a cake with a file in it, but my skills

don't extend to the kitchen," I offer with a snort. "But I am going to get you out of this."

"I'm glad you're here," he whispers, his voice tight. "I didn't do this. What they're saying. I have no idea how that stuff got in my truck."

I look over my shoulder, making sure no one is around. "I know," I say firmly. "I'm going over to Bianca's now. I'm going to get her to turn herself in. I'm going to give them everything I have."

And it still might not be enough. Though I don't say it, it hangs in the air between us.

"The worst part is, somebody went to a lot of trouble to set me up for this. I just can't figure out why. Why me?" he asks.

I feel myself pitch forward, resting my head on the vinyl siding. I've missed something.

Something important.

It hits me like a ton of bricks. I actually feel the color drain from my face.

"What is it? What's wrong?" he asks.

I open my mouth, and then close it with a snap. What can I say? I can't just accuse someone. Not without hard proof.

"I think I know who did this," I hiss. "I need to get to Bianca, but I think I know who did it all."

It's so obvious now. Like a huge puzzle, one piece fits, then suddenly, everything else falls into place and you step back, seeing the whole picture, feeling like an idiot for not seeing it before.

It's not a pretty one.

"I have to go," I say apologetically.

"No, Farris. Wait! If you know who did this, go tell one of the MPs or something!" His voice is high with urgency.

"No. I need proof first. I'll be back as soon as I can."

TWENTY

I DRIVE ACROSS BASE IN A DAZE, PULLING UP OUTSIDE Bianca's house and slamming the car into park. I'm at her door without knowing exactly how I got there, restraining myself from pounding on it. I ring the doorbell, shifting impatiently.

Bianca pulls the door open. "Hey, Farris. What's up?"

"I need to see your computer."

She leans back. "Excuse me?"

I push past her and step into the house. "Oliver's been arrested."

She closes the door behind me, her voice still wary. "Yeah, I heard. Gossip travels fast."

I turn to look at her, scanning the room as I move to make sure no one else is in earshot. "I know you're the one that hacked the squadron, Bianca. I want to know if you planted the explosives, or if someone else did it for you," I say flatly.

Her expression twists, eyebrows rising. "You're insane. I didn't do anything."

She moves to walk away but I stop her with a hand on her arm, pulling the flash drive from my pocket with the other and holding it up. "I can prove it. I hacked your Omega Portal user account and traced the threatening email and the virus back to Splice. You can talk to me, or we can call the cops right now and I'll hand them everything."

She stares at me for a minute, her mouth hanging half open. "I... I didn't do any of that. I only got on to do research for that stupid paper."

I level a gaze at her. "The jpeg you sent had an Ouroboros virus encrypted inside it. I saw the code. It's what infected the system, and I'm betting it's what brought down that plane yesterday too. The only thing I can't figure out is the explosion."

She walks past me into her living room, sinking onto the arm of her leather sofa. "It wasn't me. The whole Omega Portal thing was Reid's idea. I told him about my project idea, and he told me where I could find people who might be willing to talk. He set it all up; even let me use his username and password to access the chat rooms." She rubs her face in her hands. "I didn't even know about the other stuff. And I had nothing to do with the explosion."

My heart sinks like a lead weight in my chest. I assumed he'd set the explosion, setting Oliver up to take the blame. I never imagined he was behind everything. It's clever, I have to admit. Basically the same principal as having multiple sets of fingerprints on a gun. Even if the Feds manage to put it all together and catch up with the hacker, all trails will lead straight back to Bianca. Too naive to cover her tracks, too smart to claim she couldn't have done it.

"Here's what you're going to do," I say, handing her the drive. "You're going to go over to the Provost Marshal's office right now and tell them exactly what you just told me. Give them this."

She shakes her head. "What if they don't believe me?"

"I'll be there soon to back you up, I promise. But first, I'm going to go over to Reid's house and see if I can get my hands on his computer. If he accessed the Omega Portal at all, there may still be evidence on his hard drive. But if he thinks someone might be onto him, he could wipe the whole thing, and then it's his word against yours."

Nodding slowly, she takes the drive. "Yeah, ok."

I put a hand on her shoulder. "It's gonna be alright."

She wipes away a tear as it falls from her eye. "I never thought he'd do something like this to me. I thought he was a nice guy."

I offer her what I hope is a reassuring smile. "We all did."

Me most of all.

My mouth is dry as I walk up the front steps and knock on Reid's door. No answer. No cars in the driveway. Walking over to where the garage is attached to the house, I peek in the window. No sign of Reid's scooter, no movement of any kind. His parents, probably still out of town, will have no idea what their son has done.

My frustration spiking, I kick the garage door and it shakes with the impact. I should have seen it sooner, should have at least suspected. But he'd won me over with his story of being shunned and bullied, making himself a kindred spirit, someone who could understand me in ways other people can't. Now, I can't help but wonder if it'd all been a lie. Every moment we spent together rides through my brain and I find myself questioning each word, each look, each subtle tick, searching for some warning sign.

Trying not to look suspicious, I walk over to the side yard and reach over the fence, feeling for the lock on the other side. I slide the bolt to the side and the gate swings open. Closing it behind me, I sneak around the house. The sliding glass door in the kitchen is unlocked. Lucky me.

I move quickly through the house and into Reid's bedroom. It's neat, recently cleaned and vacuumed, his blankets draped perfectly across his bed, his pillows just so. But there's no computer on the desk. I swear out loud and hastily begin opening drawers, rummaging through the clothes inside. I open his closet, his perfectly stacked shoe boxes, and then crouch down to look under his bed. Nothing. I roll back on my heels, folding my hands under my chin, still crouched beside his bed.

Something catches my eye as I start to stand up. It's the corner of a yellow notebook sticking out from under the mattress.

I run my hand under the mattress and come out with a legal pad.

Moving to his desk, I pull out the chair and sit down, flipping through pages and pages of chemistry notes. About halfway through, I find what I'm looking for. It is a page folded neatly in half. I unfold it and struggle to understand what I'm seeing. It is a chemical formula with intricate instructions for inducing crystallization.

My mouth forms a silent *O* as I realize what the formula is for. It's directions for making ammonium chloride, a combination of chlorine and ammonia. A very dangerous combination.

A voice from the doorway startles me. "If you wanted to spend time in my bedroom, you could have just asked."

Nearly falling out of the chair, I leap to my feet, clutching the notebook and pushing the chair between us. Reid leans against the doorjamb, picking at the paint with his fingernail. His expression is placid in a way that manages to be both neutral and absolutely terrifying. Unsure how to handle the situation, I decide to try for humor.

"Jeez, Reid, why can't you just keep porn under your bed like every other teenage boy on the planet?"

He looks at me flatly, his face flushing with the beginnings of real anger. "Why are you here, Farris?"

"I talked to Bianca today. She told me the whole story. What I really don't get is why?" I ask, backing away slowly until the bump of my back against the wall tells me I have nowhere else to go. Reaching into my pocket, I feel for my phone and hit what I pray is the redial button as he starts talking again.

He rolls his eyes. "Sometimes you can be really dense, you know that?"

I narrow my eyes. "Is this because I chose Oliver?"

"No, Miss Egomaniac. But that didn't win you any points. No, this is about much more than that."

"Enlighten me then."

He looks at me like I'm dumb. "If you're looking for a tedious villainy monologue, you're not going to get one."

"You could have killed your own parents."

He shrugs. "They aren't really here anyway. Losing them wouldn't alter my life at all, except that I wouldn't have to listen to their constant whining about how much they miss their carefree, pre-Reid lives."

The last puzzle piece clicks into place. The two

chairs in the theater room, the lack of family photos in the house. I wonder what else they had done that had made him like this—to push him to this point. He isn't just being pushed around at school—that's bad enough. He's an outcast, unwanted in his own home.

"Couldn't you just be a normal human being and talk to them about it?" My voice rises now. "I mean, I get it. They hurt your feelings, but damn, dude."

"Oh, I tried that. It earned me a slap in the face and a lecture about being ungrateful. You know officers aren't supposed to fraternize. When my mom found out she was carrying me, it was too late to terminate the pregnancy. She and my dad got married, but neither of them were about to retire. They love flying. It's all they ever wanted to do. I was just a complication in their lives."

His face falls and for the briefest flicker of a moment, I feel sorry for him. Then I stiffen. "Oh please, spare me your sob story. Everybody has issues. Not all of us resort to crashing seventy-million-dollar airplanes for attention."

He glares at me, so I continue. "Derek's stepdad beats the shit out of him, Bianca is miserably in love with the girl who can't keep her eyes off you, and Oliver's trying to keep people from finding out he's got bipolar disorder. Life is shitty, Reid. Get over it."

Reid clenches his fists. "You don't know what it's like."

"Well, cry me a river. Do you feel better now that you've had your little Oprah moment? News flash, I give zero fucks why you did this. *But I'm damn sure going to make sure you never do it again,*" I fire back.

He continues as if I hadn't spoken. "You know, maybe if you'd picked *me,* I would have been more careful about making sure your dad didn't get hurt."

I'm genuinely stunned for a minute, then I want nothing more than to lunge for him and scratch his eyes out. Only the memory of him putting the ninja on Oliver stops me. In hand-to-hand, I'm outmatched. I need an exit, or a weapon.

My eyes dart around the room, searching. The only way out is the door behind Reid. Not good.

"Look, Reid, you have to turn yourself in." I let my voice drop into a soft, almost concerned tone, not so much because I think he'll listen to me, but because I'm trying to formulate an escape plan.

"Why? The police have their man." He smiles cruelly. "And once things go back to normal, I'll do it all again. Only this time, there won't be any warnings. And there won't be any mistakes."

My mind reels. "Except Bianca is already at the Provost Marshal's office, with her laptop and my file, telling them everything. By now, they already know what you did. They could be here any minute."

God, I hope that's true.

His face falls, rage flickering behind his glasses. He obviously hadn't counted on that.

"I'll figure something out," he says confidently. "Besides, it's her word against mine."

"What am I? Chopped liver?" I ask, holding up the notepad. "Oh yeah, and I have this."

He shakes his head. "Sorry, Farris. But neither you nor that are leaving this house."

Then he lunges, his fingers slicing through the air like talons, grasping for the notebook. I lean to the left, rolling onto his bed and trying to spring over him. Just when I think I'll make it to the door, his hand clamps down around my ankle and pulls me down mid-jump. I hit the edge of the bed and roll off, smacking my head on the frame as I go down.

TWENTY-ONE

STARS EXPLODE BEHIND MY EYES AS THE CONCUSSION reverberates though my skull. I can't see, but I feel his weight on top of me. He's fast, too fast. I try in vain to smack him away.

"You can't beat me, Farris." Leaning forward so I can feel his breath on my face, he hisses. "You're only hurting yourself."

I wedge my arms under his chest and try without success to push him off me.

"Oh, come on. You wanted me to kiss you, remember?" he says, breathlessly. "That night at the park. I saw it in your eyes. That's the night I thought that maybe, just maybe, you could understand. But then it was over. But you understand now, don't you?"

When he presses his mouth over mine, I gag. I grab his hair to pull his face off me, but he catches my wrists and holds them in a viselike grip. So I do the only thing I can think of. I open my mouth just a fraction, suck in his bottom lip, and bite down. Hard.

The taste of copper pennies floods my mouth as he screams and pulls back. Blood flows down his chin and drips onto my chest. I cough and spit the blood out, turning onto my side. In the scuffle, my cell phone has fallen out of my pocket and landed on the floor across from me. I reach out for it.

I don't get far.

I don't see the punch coming. It hits me on the right cheek and pain explodes, as if the impact has shattered every bone in my face. There's more blood in my mouth, but this time, it's my own.

Another punch, this time to the other side of my face, sends me reeling. The pain is sharp and relentless. Tears well up in my eyes, flowing down my cheeks as he grabs my T-shirt from the front. I bring my hands up to try to fight him off, scratching and punching, but my arms are like jelly. No matter how hard I try, I can't defend myself. He nuzzles his face into my neck as he holds my shirt, stretching the fabric as he wraps it around his fists. He kisses me. Licks me. Somehow, I find my voice and I scream. I scream and scream, until my throat is raw and no more sound will come, praying someone will hear, praying someone will help me.

I don't actually expect someone to.

He eases back just a fraction, just enough for me to see the morbid smile on his face. There's a loud crack, right before Reid slumps forward onto me, dead weight. Through my watery eyes, I make out the shape of a person standing over him like an avenging angel. She's holding a long, wooden baseball bat.

Georgia.

Her golden hair hangs loose around her flushed face. Together, we roll him off me. She pulls me up to standing, hugging me tightly and rubbing my back while I wipe the blood and tears from my face with the back of my hands.

"Shhh. It's okay. Shhh," she soothes.

When I'm finally able to breathe again, I lean back. Reid lies crumpled on the floor, his glasses askew. There's blood on his face and dripping down the back of his neck where Georgia smashed him with the bat she still holds in her left hand.

"I thought he was going to kill me! How'd you find me?" I ask, still shaky but quickly recovering.

She shakes her head. "I was in the office, waiting to see Oliver, when Bianca came in. As soon as she came in, she told me what was happening before they even took her statement. I rushed right over," she explains. "Saw your car, heard you screaming. Luckily, I had this in the trunk."

"Very luckily," I say, bending to retrieve the notebook from where it's fallen on the floor. I straighten my clothes as best I can and rake my fingers through my hair, wincing at the pain in my face.

"It's not." She hesitates, frowning. "It's my fault. Oliver wanted to tell you, but I wouldn't let him."

I look at her, not sure if it is the concussion, or if she's just not making sense.

She sighs. "The thing is, two years ago, Reid had come over. I was used to it. We were friends; he came over all the time. I never thought he'd..." She bites her lip. "He tried to force himself on me. Oliver came home just in time." The side of her mouth perks up. "And he beat the living shit out of him. He wanted me to tell someone, press charges, but I was too embarrassed. I made him promise never to tell anyone."

She looks up, her eyes searching mine. "So it's partly my fault. If I'd let Ollie tell you the truth, you'd have known what he was really like. I'm sorry for that."

"Oliver knew Reid was dangerous and he tried to warn me. I just didn't listen. That's on me, not you," I say, tapping the notebook on my leg. "But right now, we need to get this to the MPs."

She turns, stepping out of the room just ahead of me.

Without warning, a hand grabs my shoulder from behind and spins me around. Reflexively, I draw my arm back and let it uncoil into Reid's already bloody face. He falls backward into his dresser and slides down onto the floor.

Georgia is back in the doorway, bat firmly in her grasp. "Oh. Nice right hook."

I flex my hand, pretty sure I've broken something. "Thanks."

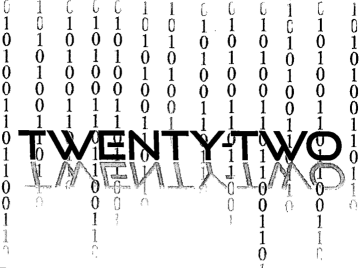

TWENTY-TWO

THE ADRENALINE RUSH WEARS OFF BEFORE THE ambulance even pulls into the hospital, leaving me feeling drained, heavy. Just walking in feels like forcing my way through quicksand, one slow, aching step at a time. They offer me a wheelchair, but I refuse, knowing that if I stop moving, even for a moment, I'll sink into shock.

Oliver's at the hospital with his parents when we get there. The EMTs had gotten to the house relatively quickly once we finally managed to convince the 911 operator that it was not, in fact, a prank and that we had just been attacked by the person responsible for crashing a seventy-million-dollar military jet. In hindsight, we should have just told them the house was on fire or something.

Still, I didn't expect them to spring Ollie quite so soon, but I've never been so glad to see anyone in my entire life. I want to rush over to him, but the corpsman ushers me straight into my room, refusing to let anyone in until I've seen the doctor.

Hours later, I'm sitting upright, tucked into a slim, hard bed while the doctor takes my vitals for the third time. I'm sore, a little shaky, and a little dizzy, but I keep trying to convince him that a double cheeseburger will fix that. He has the nurse bring me lime Jell-O instead.

Georgia is in and out of the hospital in record time. The perks of having a doctor for a father, and, you know, of not being mildly concussed or needing x-rays on a potentially broken hand.

Dr. Knight comes in to check on me after a bit. He's a kind man with Georgia's eyes and Ollie's smile, and just having him in the room relaxes me. He tells me the Marshal's office released Oliver with apologies as soon as they received word from the MPs about Reid.

He thanks me and asks me if I need anything.

Five minutes later, Oliver is at my door with a greasy fast food bag in hand.

God bless that boy.

Oliver holds my hand from the moment they let him in to see me, right up until they wheel my bed into a room with my dad, but even then, he won't leave my side. He sits on my left and Dad sits on my right as I recount the entire story, glossing over Reid's attack on me as much as possible, hoping I will never have to tell it again.

Dad and Oliver both tense at the end, squeezing my hands in turn—which really hurts my already badly bruised, but apparently not broken, knuckles.

I lay in bed for a while, sipping ice water out of a massive pink jug with a straw poking out of the lid. The nurses check on me often, waiting to see if I go into shock or something, I think. I'm determined not to give them the satisfaction.

"What were you thinking?" Oliver asks when my dad leaves to sign some paperwork.

"Don't be angry," I beg. "It's been a really long day." I rub my eyes, trying not to pull out my IV. Dad's twenty-four hours are up, but I'm in for the night.

He stares at me wordlessly, awaiting an explanation.

I sigh. "Don't look at me like that. I did what I had to. Reid would have gotten away with it all if I hadn't." I take another drink.

Oliver shakes his head. "You risked your life. I mean, he could have killed you, Farris."

I rest my head back against the pillows. "Hey, you're not telling me anything I don't know."

He smiles. "Would you like me to tell you something you might not know?"

I glance up at him, studying his face, hoping whatever he's about to say isn't bad news. I don't think I can handle any more bad news today. "Sure."

"Well," he begins, leaning over me and brushing the hair back from my face. "There's this girl. She's kind of broken, and kind of messy, and I'm hopelessly tangled up in her."

With that, he lowers himself, kissing me gently on the forehead. "And I'd yell at her for being reckless, but something tells me she'd do it again anyway."

I smile, grazing a single finger along the line of his jaw. "Bet your ass I would."

EPILOGUE

MOST OF THE TIME, MY DREAMS ARE JUST REGULAR dreams. Sometimes, however, they're the old nightmares, only with a new element. Reid's face. Occasionally, it's the kind, friendly face I still half expect to see at school, smiling at me during lunch or when I pass his old locker. More often, it's the angry, twisted, bloody face of the person who viciously attacked me, the person who blew up an airplane and sent my dad and many others to the hospital. To be honest, I think the smiling face bothers me more.

Ironically, Reid gets exactly what he wanted. The judge gives his parents two options: one of them can retire and stay home with him on house arrest, or they can let him go to juvenile detention at Seymour Johnson Air Force Base. So Reid is spending his days on house arrest, hopefully getting the treatment he needs. I haven't seen or spoken to him since that day, though Kayla has, and she tells me he's better. Calmer. Happier. I don't know if I'll ever be able to look at him again. I'm not sure I want to. Maybe that makes me a bad person. Maybe it just makes me human.

Oliver has taken over being my lab partner, and we quickly fall into a nice, normal routine. No one really knows the whole story of what happened, and I'm fine with that. I write a story about it for the school paper, glossing over the more private aspects. It's a story about a young man, wounded by his parents' choices, who was driven to desperate measures just to make them see him. The editor refuses to publish the piece, of course, but offers me a spot on the paper anyway. I turn her down, and honestly, I'm still not sure why.

Georgia and I enroll in kickboxing classes at the base gym. Sometimes, when I have the nightmares, I call her, and she talks about some random piece of gossip until I feel better. We never speak about what happened that day. We're both getting over it, and that's enough.

Oliver turns out to be the best boyfriend a girl could ask for, although we have to decide by paper, rock, scissors who gets to drive every time we go out. I win a lot.

The lunch table goes through an interesting convergence. After Oliver and Georgia start sitting with Derek, Kayla, and me, the rest of their friends slowly follow suit and now we're a big, weird clique of our own. Cole even procures a vintage Save Ferris

T-shirt and wears it often to annoy me. I secretly love it. Will wonders never cease?

Derek and Kayla are ever the perfect couple. Where she's loud and outrageous, he's calm and cool. Ice complementing her fire. For her birthday, I get them tickets to a showing of *The Rocky Horror Picture Show* at the Armory in DC. A whole night with people who love black corsets and fishnets as much as they do. Of course, they drag me along and I have to admit, it's the most fun I've had in a while, though I'm washing off glitter for the better part of a week..

Oh, and a strange thing happens. Someone sends an anonymous email to Child Services on base about Derek's stepdad, who is soon forced to start anger management therapy. Now every week, Derek has to go talk to a shrink about how things are going and give a report. He never says anything to me about it, but he seems less afraid to go home now. Small miracles.

We are settling into a nice groove when Dad deploys in October. It's hard for me to see him go, but I know from experience that six months isn't really that long. Plus, he assures me that while the squad is flying combat missions, he'll be firmly on the ground, well away from the heavy action. I suppose it was the best I can hope for, considering. Am I still scared of losing him? You bet. But I'm not paralyzed by the fear of it. I have lots of people I love and who love me, to help me shoulder the burden when things get too heavy, and that makes all the rest worthwhile.

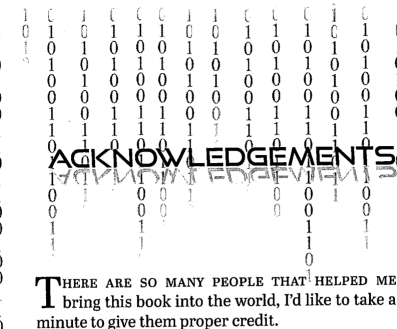

ACKNOWLEDGEMENTS

THERE ARE SO MANY PEOPLE THAT HELPED ME bring this book into the world, I'd like to take a minute to give them proper credit.

To Sidge 2.0, in particular, thanks for sending me in the right direction with the hacker stuff. I'm sure I still screwed up plenty, but at least I know what an IP address is now.

And of course, big thanks to my writers club, CJ, Lisa, Rodney, Aimee, Gabby. Thanks for being an inspiration always.

Thanks to my family, who spent spring break locked in the living room while I finished this book. You guys sacrifice a lot so I can do the stuff I love, and I want you to know that you are my heart.

Thanks to the team at Clean Teen Publishing, who, as always, are not only amazing humans, but are people I'm glad to call friends.

Thank you to the readers, bloggers, and fans who pick up books, love them, and give them homes inside your heart.

And a special thanks to those serving and who have served, and to their families, who sacrifice and risk themselves to keep us safe from those who would harm us. You are truly heroes.

Semper Fi.

ABOUT THE AUTHOR

S HERRY D. FICKLIN IS A FULL TIME WRITER FROM Colorado where she lives with her husband, four kids, two dogs, and a fluctuating number of chickens and house guests. A former military brat, she loves to travel and meet new people. She can often be found browsing her local bookstore with a large white hot chocolate in one hand and a towering stack of books in the other. That is, unless she's on deadline at which time she, like the Loch Ness monster, is only seen in blurry photographs.

CPSIA information can be obtained
at www.ICGtesting.com
Printed in the USA
FSOW01n0001200815
9965FS